Deceit Can Be Deadly

By Ron Day

Morris Publishing Australia

http://morrispublishingaustralia.com

i

Deceit
Can Be Deadly

By Ron Day

ISBN: 978-0-6454766-6-8

The right of Ron Day to be identified as the author of this work has been asserted by him.

Dedication

Dedicated to my lovely wife, Elaine, who supports my writing endeavours with a smile and words of praise. I also appreciate her assistance with editing, which she does with consummate skill.

I would like also to dedicate this, the second in a series of murder mysteries, to those who delight in reading these mysteries, perhaps with a glass of wine in hand, and who try to guess the perpetrator before the climactic scene.

Chapter One

I twirled the Cabernet Sauvignon wine around the glass to release the esters. I held the glass by its stem to my nose to inhale the flavours. Nothing much at all. I took a sip. Blaah!!! It was horrible. It tasted like a very old, oxidised vinegar. Yuk!!! I spat it out and reached for a glass of water to cleanse my mouth.

Alec looked at me in surprise from behind the bar. 'What's the matter, Sean?'

'This wine tastes like sour old vinegar.'

'Vinegar? But that's one of our top wines.'

He poured a small amount of the wine from the same bottle into his glass. He sniffed and wrinkled his nose in distaste. He took a small sip. He spluttered and spat it out.

'This isn't our wine. What's going on?' he said.

'Your label is on the bottle,' I pointed out.

'Label or not, this putrid wine is not ours.'

He reached for another bottle from the same case, opened it and poured a sample into a fresh glass. He sniffed and tasted with disgust. 'This is definitely not our wine. Someone has sabotaged this case,' he shouted in anger.

Alec lifted the internal phone and dialled the Chief Winemaker. When the call was answered he said, 'Can you come into the Cellar Door Sales area straight away, please, Mark.'

I was sitting on a tall bar stool with my arm resting on the long timber bar. Along it I could see several sinks and taps, carefully arranged wine bottles, plates of dry biscuits, and cut pieces of fruit and vegetables.

While we waited for Mark, I looked around the Cellar Door Sales room. Tables and chairs waited for visitors to come to taste and buy wines. Quiet music added an ambiance to encourage visitors to loosen their wallets and purse strings. The walls were decorated with wine competition awards and large posters describing the characteristics of wine varieties. A fire spread welcome warmth from a large stone fireplace at one end of the room.

Mark bustled into the tasting room, a concerned expression on his face. 'How can I help you,' he enquired of Alec.

'Try this wine and tell me what you think.'

Mark rotated the glass, sniffed, tasted, and spat the wine into a nearby sink in disgust. 'That's awful. Show me the label.'

Alec turned the bottle, so the label faced Mark. 'That batch only came from the district wine storage centre yesterday. Dave delivered it towards evening, so I hadn't time to check it.'

'Right,' said Alec. 'We'll both go and talk with Dave tomorrow morning. 'You can come too, Sean, if you would like. I may need your forensic accounting skills in solving this riddle.'

So, no murder to solve this time, just a labelling mix-up, I thought. *Although the look on Alec's face tells me we may have a murder when he finds out who has done this.*

'What riddle?' asked Kate as she walked through the door, still dressed in her riding gear.

As she walked in, Alec's daughter smiled a welcome in my direction.

She looks good in those jodhpurs, I thought. *I wonder if she will invite me for a ride sometime.*

'There's been a mix up with our best wine at the Wine Store. We are going to see Dave tomorrow to sort it out.'

She looked at me. 'Are you going?'

At my nod she smiled. 'I'm coming too.'

'If you like,' said her father. 'We may need your legal knowledge if push comes to shove.'

'I'm only halfway through my degree, but I may have learned something useful to help Sean. He's the expert at solving mysteries.'

I smiled. I had been successful with several recent business crime investigations. 'But we don't know there is anything to investigate yet. It may have just been an unfortunate mix up,' I commented.

'Mix up or deliberate sabotage, I want it sorted immediately! If any of this wine is distributed anywhere during the Food and Wine Gourmet Week in two weeks' time, our reputation will be destroyed,' Alec snarled. 'Our business will die. And we won't be around for the October Wine Competition where we normally take prizes.'

He bustled round tidying up with erratic and hurried movements before closing the Cellar Door Sales area for the day.

'Stay for dinner, Sean,' invited Kate. 'You can tell us all about your latest investigation.'

'Oi'd love to. That'd be grand,' I said, slipping into my native Dublin accent. I looked forward to spending more time with this attractive young lady. She was smart too, both qualities high on my list.

* * *

The following morning, we piled into Alec's Landcruiser, Mark with Alec in the front and Kate in the back with me. Before long Alec pulled into the drive that led to Dave's wine storage shed. The long drive meandered around a plantation of native trees and shrubs that sheltered the buildings from the view of passing motorists. We eventually came to a large open area where we could see Dave's house to the right and the large wine store and machinery shed to the left.

Alec parked near the double door and loading platform at the front of the store. There was no sign of Dave.

'He's probably doing wine deliveries,' Alec suggested.

I headed for the door, which was closed but not locked. Local winemakers often brought pallets of wine to the store or took pallets from storage when Dave was away doing deliveries or pickups. He depended on an honesty system where people were expected to leave him a note to say what they had brought or taken.

I opened one of the doors and walked in. The others hesitated for a moment but then followed me in, closing the door behind them.

This huge, air-conditioned space was crowded with pallets of wine, three pallets high in haphazard order. Each pallet held sixty-four twelve-bottle cases of wine or one hundred and twenty-eight, six-bottle cases.

'Whew,' uttered Kate. 'So much wine.'

'That's understandable,' explained her father. 'He stores excess wine for most of the wineries in the Clare Valley.'

'How do we find ours?' she asked.

'I suggest we spread out and look,' I said.

The others nodded. We each headed in a different direction.

'I've found some,' called Mark a few minutes later.

We hurried in the direction of his voice and soon stood in front of a stack three pallets high. We could see Alec's label on boxes of wine out of our reach on the top pallet.

'Too high to reach,' said Mark.

'I can fix that,' I said. 'I saw a forklift as we came in.'

'Can you drive that thing?' asked Kate with a touch of amazement in her voice.

'Done it many times,' I replied, trying not to sound too superior.

I hurried back towards the entrance and climbed into the forklift parked near the door. I turned the ignition key to start the engine then moved the lever to lift the forks off the ground. I moved the speed lever up a notch or two and trundled towards the group.

'Give me room, please,' I called as I drew close.

They stepped back quickly as I lifted the forks high enough to slide under the top pallet. I soon had the pallet on the ground.

Alec dragged a carton from the top level and broke it open. He pulled a bottle out and handed it to Mark before grabbing another for himself. He twisted the metal Stelvin cap to open it, held the bottle to his lips and took a small mouthful. He spat the wine out onto the concrete floor. 'Yuk!' he said in disgust. 'This is the crappy wine.'

'The label on this one is not quite square,' said Mark. 'It has been applied by hand, not by a bottling machine.'

'This one too,' said Alec. 'Someone has been applying our labels to someone else's poor-quality wine. They obviously want our wines to fail during Gourmet tasting and the October competition. With this wine we will become a laughingstock. Our business will be ruined.'

'How could someone else get hold of your labels?' I asked.

'That is a question we will have to ask the label printer,' said Alec with a growl. 'We'll take this carton with us. I want to mark every box on this pallet, so let's get busy and unpack them. Kate, would you please scout around and see if you can find a marking pen or two?'

'Okay, Dad,' she replied as she turned and walked away.

Soon we had sixty-four twelve-bottle cases piled around us. Kate returned with four marking pens, and we set to work drawing a large black cross on one side of each box. The boxes were soon piled back on the pallet, which I lifted into place with the forklift, minus the opened box that Mark carried to the car.

'Dad,' asked Kate. 'Do you think there might be fingerprints on those bottles?'

'Good thinking, Kate,' said Alec. 'We'll take this box to the police station to see if they can check.'

'I suggest we ask Dave how he has this pallet in his store,' I said.

'I had that thought too,' replied Alec. 'We'll catch up with him later. Let's go and talk to the police. Before we go, I'll leave a note for Dave to tell him about the pallet we have marked.'

We were soon on our way down the highway towards Clare.

* * *

We walked into the police station, Mark carrying the box. The sergeant looked up from a handful of paperwork. 'Good to see you, Alec.' A smile crossed his face when he saw the box of wine. 'Surely not a bribe.'

'No such luck, Bob. Someone has been putting our labels on putrid wine. We are hoping you have someone who can check for fingerprints.'

'Not today, mate. Our fingerprint forensics expert is on a job at Crystal Brook. I'll get him to test your wine bottles tomorrow morning. Leave your box with me and I'll attend to it.'

'Thanks, Bob, but don't let anyone else touch the bottles. We hope the fingerprints will tell us who is running this scam.'

'No worries. Consider it done.'

Alec turned to his group. 'Come on. There's nothing more we can do for the present. Let's have a coffee before we go home.'

We ordered coffee at the local coffee shop and sat in the afternoon sun. Around us on the ground lay leaves from the deciduous trees lining the street. It was good to be able to open coats and jumpers as we enjoyed an unusual touch of warmth on this late autumn day. The coffee soon arrived.

'Who is your label printer?' I asked.

'Advantage Wine Label Suppliers.'

'Where are they based?'

'Melbourne. We order all our labels through the Internet,' replied Alec.

'Does that mean anyone could order your labels?' I queried.

'That is obviously possible.'

'No security measures?'

'None that I know of,' said Alec shortly.

'Can I suggest you call them and ask who ordered your last batch of labels?'

'Good thinking, Sean. I'll do that as soon as we get home.'

* * *

When we reached the winery, Alec disappeared into his office while we gathered around the fireplace. Mark stoked the fire and added wood. Soon the flames burst into a cheery, warming, crackling glow.

'An unknown person ordered the labels over the phone three weeks ago,' announced Alec when he returned to the room. 'The person paid with a credit card on the spot. Usually, they send me an invoice.'

'Will they give you the card details?' I asked.

'Not over the phone.'

'Alec, if you give me a letter of authority, I'll fly to Melbourne tomorrow. I'll get the card details so we can

9

contact the bank. In future, I think you should insist they set up security measures. If they won't, change to a printer who will.'

'Sound advice, Sean. I'll give you a credit card to use for your airfare and expenses.'

'Thanks, Alec. Can I please use your office to book the flight and a hire car?'

Chapter Two

The next morning, I left early to drive to the Adelaide airport. The car journey from Clare to Adelaide took around an hour and a half; and the flight from Adelaide to Melbourne took about an hour.

Before lunch I had reached Melbourne Airport and climbed into my hire car. I set the GPS to the address for the printing firm and began the journey. It took some time negotiating the busy Melbourne streets, but I eventually found the printers.

A cheerful young lady greeted me at the front counter. 'How can I help you, Sir?'

'I need to speak with your manager about some wine labels you printed for Daybreak Wines in the Clare Valley in South Australia,' I said with a smile.

'I'll see if he is available,' she replied.

She lifted her desk phone, dialled an internal number, and waited. After a few moments, the phone call was answered, and she explained my reason for the visit. I could hear a voice replying but couldn't hear the words.

'He will see you shortly,' she told me.

Before long, a tall, lanky man in a grey suit appeared from his office. He held out his hand and greeted me.

'John Payne,' he said. 'Welcome to Melbourne.'

'Sean O'Connor,' I replied. 'I'm pleased you could see me so promptly.'

'Not a problem. Always pleased to meet good customers. Come into my office.'

I stepped through the doorway and took the seat offered near his desk.

'What is the reason for the visit?' he asked. 'We normally communicate via the Internet.'

I proffered the letter of authority. 'The owner, Alec Marchison, has asked me to act on his behalf in this matter.'

'What is your role?' the printer questioned.

'I am a business management consultant. I regularly audit this winery,' I explained. 'John, someone ordered a batch of their labels recently by phone and paid for them with a credit card instead of the usual process of you sending an invoice. Those labels have been attached to poor quality wine and passed off as coming from their winery. If those bottles get out, their reputation will be in tatters, and they will not need wine labels in the future. We need to identify the person and stop this scam immediately. I would like you to supply us with the details of the credit card so we can get the police to take action.'

John's face displayed amazement, then closed. 'I can't give you details like that. We have rules about privacy that preclude such action.'

'John, one of your staff took an order for Daybreak's labels by phone and accepted a credit card payment. They always order through the Internet and receive an invoice for their orders, which they pay promptly. That is the way their business with you is conducted. When the buyer offered to pay by credit card, it should have sounded alarm bells. Their privacy with you was breeched by your staff member.'

John's face grew red. 'How dare you attack my staff? You can't come in here and attack us. Get out of my office now!'

I remained seated and stared at his eyes. He shuffled in his seat uncomfortably.

'If you can't help, then I will suggest they use another printer for their labels. Not only that. We will spread the word that you don't use sufficient security measures. As I said, before taking this order and a credit card payment by phone, your staff member should have identified that this is not the usual way business with them is conducted. It is normal business practise that you would contact them when this happens, to verify that it is a genuine order.'

I sat back, trying to calm the anger I felt so I could attempt to regain a co-operative atmosphere.

John sat there like a wooden Indian. I could see signs of panic. He wasn't used to being taught his business, but I was sure he realised his staff member had made a serious mistake.

'John, I didn't come all this way to argue with you. I came hoping you would help us solve this crime without the involvement of the police. But, if necessary, I can call my very good friend Detective Inspector Ken Harris of the South Australian Crime Squad. He will call one of his Melbourne friends and have a detective here in minutes to take over this criminal investigation.'

'No police, please,' he stuttered.

'All I need are the details of the credit card and the address to which this order was sent. I will hand those details over to the police when I return to Adelaide and let them investigate locally. You don't need to be involved any further.'

John sighed. 'You win. I'll get the card and address details.'

He rose from his office chair and walked out the door. Soon I could hear filing cabinet drawers being opened and papers being shuffled. After a while, he returned to his office and handed me a piece of paper. On it were the credit card and address details I needed.

'Thank you, John. I appreciate your help,' I said sincerely. 'Can you promise me one thing?' I enquired.

'What is that?' he said shortly.

'That your staff members will be briefed never to take phone orders or credit card details for Daybreak's wine label orders in the future.'

'That will be attended to immediately.'

'Thank you.'

I held out my hand. He looked at it for a long moment, then reluctantly raised his hand to shake mine. I walked from the room. I was sure I would never be his new best friend. I would ask Alec to call him and offer his thanks too.

* * *

I climbed into the hire car and drove back to the airport. While I was waiting for my flight, I called my friend Detective Inspector Ken Harris and asked for a meeting when I returned to Adelaide.

Little more than an hour or so later I was seated in his office.

'What have you got yourself into this time?' he asked with a cheeky grin on his face.

Ken and I had worked together on several cases in the past and we had become close friends.

'No murders this time,' I replied.

His face showed disappointment. 'I don't believe it. You normally manage to work in a murder or two, just to keep me interested.'

'I'll see what I can organise for you,' I said with a grin. 'This time we are talking a business fraud case.'

I sketched out the details. 'I'm asking you to help me identify the owner of a credit card that was used to buy wine bottle labels under a false identity. That person glued my mate Alec's labels onto some substandard wine. Someone wants to ruin his business during the Clare Valley Food and Wine Gourmet Week and put him out of contention in the October Wine Competition. It threatens to put him out of business totally.'

'I get the picture. Got the card details?'

I reached into my coat pocket, pulled out the paper and handed it to Ken.

'I won't ask how you got these details.'

'Best not,' I said with a smile.

He lifted his phone and made a quick call. Shortly a policewoman walked into his office.

'How can I help, Sir?' she asked Ken.

'Find out who owns this credit card. It was used to buy wine bottle labels in Melbourne.'

'Too easy,' she said as she walked from the office.

Before long, she returned with some details on a sheet of paper. She placed it on Ken's desk near his hand.

'There is a problem, Sir,' she said.

'Which is?'

'That card is mentioned on a list of hacked card numbers.'

'Meaning?'

'Someone has procured that number through the Dark Web. The card belongs to a woman in Western Australia. I doubt she would have ordered wine labels in Melbourne.'

'Call her to make sure and treat her politely. Suggest she contacts her bank to cancel the card and the purchase.'

'Yes, Sir,' she said as she walked briskly from Ken's office.

'So, Sean, we have someone in the Clare Valley using a credit card illegally to purchase wine labels in Melbourne. What about the delivery address? Does that help us?'

'It's a Post Office mailbox number,' I replied. 'I'll have to visit the Post Office to find out who paid for that number.'

'No, mate. You've done enough. I'll call Sergeant Murray. His request will carry more clout than yours. Give me a moment.'

Ken looked up a directory and found the phone number for the Clare Police Station. I could hear the phone ringing, then a muffled voice answered.

'Hi, Bob. Ken Harris from Crime Investigations here.'

'Good afternoon, Inspector,' I heard faintly.

'I believe you know about the placement of Daybreak wine labels on dodgy wine.'

'Yes, Sir,' was his reply.

'Bob, I have Sean O'Connor here with me. I'll place you on speaker phone.'

'G'day, Sean,' he said.

'Hi, Bob,' I replied. 'Nice to talk with you again.'

'Bob, I have a job for you,' said Ken. 'Will you please go to the Post Office and ask who uses Private Box number 271?'

'271?'

'That's the one, Bob. Can you please do that right away and report back to me as soon as you can.'

'On my way now,' he replied and closed the call.

We chatted while we waited.

'Why don't you bring Mandy to the Clare Valley the weekend after next for the Food and Wine Gourmet Week? You deserve a break,' I suggested.

'Might just do that. Got a bed for us?'

'Soon find one.'

The phone rang. Ken picked up the receiver.

'Hi, Inspector. Back again.'

Ken switched to speaker phone. 'What did you find out, Bob?'

'The box was paid for by someone staying at the Clare Caravan Park. The Post Office lady said he booked it in the name of Geoff Stanley. She didn't see any ID, so she doesn't know whether that was his real ID or an assumed name. She did say she thinks he rides a motorbike. She heard a loud exhaust noise as he pulled up and again when he left. Said it sounded like a Harley. That's all I can help you with.'

'Many thanks, Bob. That's a good start with the investigation. Goodbye.'

He put the phone down.

'Need my help any further on this one?' he asked me.

'Not just yet, Ken. But I'll try to make it interesting enough to drag you out of the city.'

'Cheers, Mate,' he said as I stood and walked to the door.

'See you soon,' I said as I left his office.

Chapter Three

Back in the winery the next morning, I was besieged.

'What did you find out?' asked Alec.

'Who owns the credit card?' asked Mark

'Where were the labels delivered?' asked Kate.

'Woah!' I shouted. 'Let me catch my breath.'

They stood in a determined group anxious to hear the result of my investigations.

'Come on, Sean. Don't keep us in suspense,' urged Alec.

I smiled and said, 'Well, here goes. One... The credit card was hacked from a woman in Western Australia. Two... The labels were delivered to a private mailbox at the Clare Post Office. Three... The person who opened the mailbox said his name was Geoff Stanley. He may be a resident at the Clare Caravan Park, and he may ride a Harley motorbike.'

'Wow! How did you find all that out?' queried Kate.

'I had some help from my mate, Detective Inspector Ken Harris, in the Adelaide Crime Investigation Branch.'

'Good friend to have,' commented Alec. 'But where does that leave us?'

'With lots more to investigate,' I replied.

'Okay,' suggested Alec. 'Time to get organised. Let's sit down with a coffee and a large piece of paper. We need to devise a plan of action.'

Mark brewed some coffee and brought the cups over to a table while Alec located a large piece of paper and some pens. Kate arranged chairs around the table and shepherded me into one. Alec spread the paper and pens over the tabletop.

'Let's list each question and then brainstorm actions,' he said when we were seated.

'First question. Why would someone at the Caravan Park purchase a private mailbox?'

'Because he is working with a local winemaker,' I replied.

'How do we find out who that is?' Kate asked.

'Okay. Let's list actions,' said Alec. 'What can we do to answer those questions?'

Mark spoke up quickly. 'Put me down to visit the Caravan Park and find the person who ordered a private mailbox.'

'Be very careful, Mark,' I said. 'Someone riding a Harley and purchasing a private mailbox for a scam is likely to be a tough character operating on the wrong side of the law. I'm guessing he is being paid by a local winemaker to ruin the business.'

'I'll talk to the competition organisers and get a list of the wineries that will be competing in the Cabernet

Sauvignon category,' said Alec. 'That should narrow the possible culprits.'

'I'll see Dave and find out how that dodgy wine got into his store,' I said.

'I'll come with you, Sean,' said Kate. 'You might need a woman's charm.'

I smiled at her. 'Let's see if he is home now.'

'OK,' she replied.

'I'll go down to the Caravan Park now,' said Mark.

'And I'll see the wine-judging committee chairperson now,' said Alec.

We all rose and set off on our tasks.

Kate and I drove to Dave's wine storage area. Luckily for us, he was home. We could hear the forklift moving around in the shed. We walked to the door, pushed it open and stepped into the cool room atmosphere.

Dave spotted us, turned off the forklift and walked towards us.

'Hi Sean. Haven't seen you in a while. And you are Kate, aren't you, Alec's daughter?'

'Yes, Dave, I am. Hi.'

'How can I help you two today?' he enquired.

'Dave, we have a problem you might be able to help us with. That wine you delivered to the winery the other day was tampered with. Can you remember how it got into your store?'

22

'Daybreak?' He thought for a few moments.

We stood quietly letting him gather his thoughts.

'That was a strange one. I came back from a delivery the other day and two pallets of Daybreak wine were standing just inside the door. I thought one of their staff had left them there. I moved them into that corner over there.'

He pointed in the direction of the pallet we had discovered the previous day. 'I delivered one of those to you the other day when Mark said you were getting short.'

'Were there any delivery dockets or other identifying papers?' Kate asked.

'No. None. I was surprised because you guys are usually good at letting me know what you have done so I can keep the books straight.'

'Dave, did you get Alec's note about the second pallet?' I asked.

'Yes. I noticed the black crosses on the boxes. What are they for?'

'Someone has attached Alec's labels to crap wine. We have the police investigating it now.' I replied. 'I don't suppose you have CCTV cameras so we can view the delivery?'

'No, Sean. No such luck. I've thought about it but just haven't got around to it yet.'

'Bugger,' I said, 'We really need to know who is putting their labels on crap wine.'

'You think someone is out to get Daybreak?' he asked.

'We are sure of it. If any more wine with our labels on comes into your store without our correct documentation, can you please call and let us know straight away?'

'Sure thing. I'll do that for you.' He thought for a moment. 'Do you mean someone wants crap wine with Daybreak label on it to be spread around during the Food and Wine Gourmet Week and lodged with the judges for the October Wine Competition?'

'We are sure that is what is intended.'

'What a whacker! That's criminal!' His head shook sideways. 'He needs to be locked up.'

'He certainly does,' I replied. 'Can you just keep you ear to the ground, Dave? You know everyone in the Valley. Someone might let something slip.'

'Will do, Sean. I'll let you know if I hear anything incriminating.'

'There is one more thing, Dave,' I said. 'You delivered one of those two pallets to the winery the other day. Can you please deliver the second one asap? We don't want anyone else to get their hands on that crap wine.'

'I'll have it there this afternoon.'

We shook hands, and Kate and I took our leave.

'Do you believe him, Sean?' asked Kate as we drove back to the winery.

'Yes, I think I do. I've never experienced any dodgy business from him in the past. Wish he had CCTV cameras. That would have helped us a heap.'

As we approached the winery, we could see Alec's car in its carpark. We parked and began walking towards the Cellar Door Sales room. Mark pulled into the carpark a short time later.

As we entered the room, Alec came from his office with a sheet of paper in his hand. He greeted us and suggested we sit together to report. Mark walked in soon after and came straight to our table. We could tell from his movements that he had a big story to tell and could hardly wait to report to us about his visit.

'Go ahead, Mark. Would you like to give us your report first?' asked Alec.

'Yes, Alec. When I arrived at the caravan park, I saw three bikers sitting on their Harleys. They looked tough – leather jackets, flowing beards, lots of tats. They were drinking beer. I walked over to them and asked, "Is one of you, Geoff Stanley?" The one I took to be their leader said, "No one here of that name. What's it to you?" "What is your name," I asked. "Racoon," he answered.

'I studied his Harley. It was different to the others as it had a towbar at the back for towing a small trailer. I talked about the Post Office box and the illegal purchase of wine labels. The leader stood up and came close to me. He said, "Listen, Sonny Jim. People who come around asking questions like that are asking to be hurt.

Get your arse out of my space pronto!" He raised a fist, and I moved out of his reach as fast as I could.'

'You've stirred up a wasp's nest there,' I said.

'It was a mistake for you to go there. I wish you hadn't done that,' said Alec. 'You have made yourself a target. Now they have been identified they will probably disappear. They are probably the ones who purchased the labels, but I'm sure they did it for someone else. Make sure you always have other staff near you and keep the winery doors locked as much as you can.'

'Okay, Alec. I'll take care.'

Alec turned to me. 'What did you discover from talking with Dave?'

'The two pallets of mislabelled wine were left inside his store when he was away doing deliveries. No documentation was left with them, so he has no idea who put them there,' I replied. 'I asked him to deliver the second of those two pallets here this afternoon so we can make sure no one else gets their hands on it.'

'Good thinking, Sean. Well, we haven't progressed very far yet,' said Alec. 'I managed to get a list of the winemakers who will submit Cabernet for tasting during the festival, and who will be submitting wine to the judges in October. There are eight wineries on their list including us. I also made them promise to only include wine in the judging that I have personally delivered. I told them why.'

'What was their response,' I asked.

'They were disgusted that someone would go to such lengths to discredit us. We have their full support.'

'Good,' said Kate.

'I have a suggestion, Alec,' I said. 'We could visit those seven wineries to taste their best Cabernets tomorrow. We may be able to sense some vibes from the guilty winemaker.'

'I don't have any other ideas to progress our investigation. I'll go along with that. What do you think, Kate?'

'There's no way you are going to leave me out of this trip,' she said with a smile. 'Sounds like a super idea.'

'Mark, would you like to join us tomorrow?'

'I'd love to join you, but I have some Shiraz that needs to be bottled. I also need to place an order for some of our chemicals. Our stocks are getting low.'

'Okay. Until tomorrow then,' said Alec.

I stood to walk to the door when Alec called to me.

'Before you go, Sean,' said Alec. 'I have another problem that you may be able to help me with.'

I turned to him, a questioning expression on my face. I thought we had enough problems already. 'What is it?'

'I've had a text from our caterers who normally provide food for our customers during the Gourmet Week. They have had a death in the family and have cancelled for this year. We have advertised our food and wine events but suddenly have no one to provide the food. I don't suppose in your travels you have come across a catering company who would come at a moment's notice?'

I took a deep breath while my mind raced through possibilities. Then I stopped with a jerk. *Of course*. There was one outstanding caterer I knew who not only produced great food but also had the resources to help with our current enquiries. *Will he come? Of course he will when I ask him.*'

'Alec, I have a close friend who is one of the top restauranteurs in Adelaide. His restaurant produces some of the best Italian meals I have ever tasted.'

Alec's face lit up. 'Do you think he might come on such short notice?'

'We can only ask. I'll call him right away.'

'Please do, Sean. Use my office. Make all the arrangements. I'll be happy to foot the bill.'

I walked into Alec's office, lifted his phone, and dialled Marcello's number.

'*Pronto.*'

'Marcello, it's Sean.'

'Sean, *amico mio.* How can I help?'

I explained the problem and asked for his help.

'But of course, *fratello mio.* What are brothers for? It will be good for some of my team to work in a winery. More experience makes better workers. I will put Angelo, one of my sons, in charge. He will make sure everything is done professionally.' He paused, 'But no murders? You are not being threatened?'

'No, Marcello, but I need the help of your clever nieces and nephews who can make a computer sing. Is it possible they can do some checking for me?'

'*Si. Naturalemente*. Email me details.'

'Thank you, Marcello. I will do that today. *Ciao*.'

'*Ciao*,' he replied.

I put the phone down, opened a computer and began sketching out the details of our wine problem.'

'Alec,' I called. 'Who are the best Cabernet winemakers in the Valley?'

He walked into the office and placed his sheet of paper on the desk in front of me. 'These are the ones who could have a reason for wanting to put us out of business and to not win the championship. I trust most of them, but you never know. Winning the championship means prestige, and it also means money from increased sales.'

I entered the details into my email to Marcello and sent it on its way.

'Who was that to?' Alec asked. 'It won't be broadcast widely, will it?'

'It is quite safe,' I answered. 'I am asking for help from a very close friend who has some amazing resources at his fingertips.'

I didn't mention that my friend the restauranteur was also a Mafia boss with a team of relatives who could find out anything about anyone he asked them to investigate. We needed that assistance right now.

Chapter Four

The following morning Alec, Kate and I set out on our winery tour. We were looking forward to this chance to sample some of the opposition wine.

The Clare Valley has the ideal climate and soil types to grow very good quality wine. The south of the valley has cooler weather and soil types that favour white wines, particularly Riesling that takes out prizes at wine shows, even in Germany where some of the most prestigious Rieslings in the world are grown.

The north of the valley has more of the terra rosa red clay that grows some fine Shiraz and Cabernet Sauvignon grapes. Some of the locals will boast that these are also world beaters.

I licked my lips as we approached the first winery on Alec's list. We walked in, our ears and eyes attuned to any vibes that suggested this winery was the one attacking us.

'Hello, Alec,' welcomed the owner when we walked in the door of the Cellar Door Sales area. His face beamed with pleasure at the sight of one of his old winemaking friends.

No suggestion of an enemy here, I thought.

'Good morning, Kevin. We are just doing the rounds. I'm showing my daughter Kate and my friend Sean some of the best wineries in the valley. They are keen to taste other wines to compare it with ours. Hope you don't mind.'

'Mind? I'm delighted that you think we are in the prestige bracket. We like to think our wine is quite good, but I am sure it doesn't match yours.'

'Rubbish, Kevin. You know your wine is as good as ours. The only difference might be in the oaking. Can we taste your best Cabernet?'

'Of course you can. It will be my pleasure to pour you each a glass.'

'Just a taste, Kevin please. Not a full glass. We have to be able to drive home.'

Kevin smiled as he opened one of his best Cabernets and poured generous tasting amounts into three glasses.

We each lifted our glass to our nose to sense the esters such as the aroma of fresh mown grass, before taking a small mouthful and rolling it around our palate sensing for the acids, tannins and fruit flavours found in good Cabernet. True tasters spit the wine out into spittoons, but we swallowed to experience sublime enjoyment as the mellow juice found its way slowly down the little red lane.

'Beautiful nose,' commented Alec.

'Lovely mouthfeel,' I added. 'I could sense the hole in the middle that all good Cabernets have.'

'Gorgeous wine,' said Kate. 'Dad, this one is very good.'

Alec smiled. 'Don't give Kevin too much praise. He will burst with pride.'

'No chance of that, but I appreciate your comments. It validates the qualities we try to build into the wine.'

'Thank you, Kevin,' said Alec. 'We must go but many thanks for letting us taste your best.'

'My pleasure. Come again soon.'

We left, feeling we could cross Kevin off our list.

'Six to go,' said Alec as he backed the vehicle from the parking space and headed to the next winery.

As he drove, Alec mused, thinking aloud. 'I don't see why anyone in the Valley would need to go to such lengths to discredit us. All they have to do is spend a little more time in the vineyard, taking better care of their grapevines and experimenting with oak treatments. It wouldn't take much to produce a wine that could beat us in the wine show.'

'This speaks of criminal behaviour,' I suggested. 'I think there is something much bigger at play that we are missing at the moment.'

'Well, let's keep going. From now on we will use the spittoon and not swallow any wine. We need to keep ourselves as sharp as we can. Look for something – anything that seems dodgy. We must be able to spot a clue.'

The next two wineries were just like the first. The staff were friendly and went out of their way to make us feel comfortable. Like Kevin, they seemed glad to offer us a taste of their best Cabernets and pleased at our positive responses. Most of the winefolk in the Clare Valley are like family. They are open and hospitable, going out of their way to make others feel welcome. Our first break came at the fourth winery.

As we walked into the Cellar Door Sales room of the Lone Dog Winery, the owner saw us coming and made a hurried exit into his office.

'Where's Nigel going in such a hurry?' Alec asked. 'He seems like he doesn't want to talk with us.'

We stepped up to the bar and asked one of the staff if we could taste some of their Cabernets. He looked sideways as if seeking permission from Nigel. Not seeing his boss, he pulled himself together and reached for a bottle of Cabernet and some tasting glasses.

'Is this your best Cabernet,' asked Alec.

'No,' was the brisk reply. 'We don't open that in the tasting room.'

'Not even for another winemaker?' Alec pressed.

'No. The boss forbids us to show that wine to anyone. He is the only one to do that.'

'I saw Nigel go into his office when we came in. Would you mind asking him if we can try the best?'

The staff member turned reluctantly towards the office, walked to the door, knocked, and poked his head in to ask the question.

'No!' we heard exploding through the doorway. A few undecipherable words followed that.

The young chap almost leapt backwards in fright. Pulling the door closed, he turned back to the bar.

'The boss says he is too busy to see you today and doesn't want you to taste his best Cabernet without being there to talk you through it.'

'That's unusual for Nigel,' Alec said. 'Normally he is much friendlier. We'll come back another time when he is not so busy.'

We returned to the vehicle and climbed in.

'Number one suspect,' I said. 'But what is he so jumpy about?'

'It is a stressful time as we tidy up loose ends after vintage and prepare for the Food and Wine Gourmet Week,' explained Alec, 'but we all go through it and try to keep calm. There is something bothering Nigel. He can be a moody bugger. Gets a bee in his bonnet sometimes about little issues.'

'Should we keep him on our list?' I asked.

'I suppose so,' answered Alec, 'but I'd be surprised if he has anything to do with our problems.'

'Three wineries to go,' said Kate. 'I wonder what they will be like?'

The next two were friendly and helpful like the first three.

As we headed for the last winery on Alec's list, he said despondently, 'We've tried some tasty wines and spoken with some friendly winemakers. Only one suspicious winery so far. I can't imagine what has got into Nigel. He has problems of some kind. I'd hate to believe he has been sabotaging us, but I guess it is possible.'

We drove into the last winery on our list. There were very few vehicles in the car park.

'This is a popular winery,' said Alec. 'I expected the carpark to be full.'

We walked into the Cellar Door Sales area and were surprised to see only one person behind the bar.

'Hi,' said Alec. 'Steve, isn't it?'

'Yes, Alec. Welcome to Top of the Hill winery.'

'Where is everyone? Has Kurt given them the day off?'

'No. The Boss is having money worries and has put everyone else off.'

'Sacked them?'

'Afraid so.'

'I thought this was the wealthiest winery in the Valley,' said Alec.

'We all thought so but a couple of weeks ago the Boss sold his special model Jaguar. Now he has a second-hand Mazda. That's a big step down for him.'

'Can we taste some of his best Cabernets?'

'Sure, Alec. But we don't have much left here. He's been shipping a lot of it to Sydney. They must pay more for it over there.'

'Doesn't his son go to a fancy college in Sydney?' asked Alec.

'Yes. The rumour is that his son has got himself into gambling debt, but don't tell anyone I said that.'

'Is Kurt here today?'

'No, Alec. He left on business early this morning. He didn't say when he would be back.'

'Well. Let's sample some of the good stuff,' said Alec.

'Okay. Sit yourselves down and I'll do my best to look after you.'

Steve fetched a selection of bottles and some tasting glasses, and we set to work tasting and spitting.

'It's good wine, Steve. Do you get involved in wine making?' asked Alec.

'Yes, I look after the pumps and other machinery. I help with the wine making and get to taste blends when they need another opinion. I've gained my winemaking qualifications so it's good to be able to put some of that learning into practice. I like working here, but its changing. Since the money problems started a few weeks ago, it's been going downhill fast. I'm not sure how much longer my job will last.'

'Steve,' said Alec. 'I know you are a good worker, and honest too, in my opinion. If you lose this job, come and see me first. I think we can find a place for you.'

'Thank you, Alec. I appreciate that. If I'm put off, or if the tension here grows any worse, I'll be on your doorstep the next day.'

'Good lad.'

We thanked Steve and walked back to the car.

'Something strange is going on there,' I commented. 'I can't imagine why a successful winery like that should be having financial problems. I suggest we keep that one on our list. Two out of seven, is my count.'

'I've never had any problems with Kurt in the past, but money worries can make people do strange things,' replied Alec.

'What do you think, Kate?' I asked.

She smiled at me for including her in the conversation. 'I think we should also include number five.'

'Number five?' I queried. 'Over the Edge Winery? Why do you say that?'

'The owner, Cynthia, wasn't it? She was so smarmy.'

'Smarmy?'

'She was playing up to you two men. She sucked you in and told you a pack of lies. I don't believe anything she said. Couldn't you tell she was pumping you for information?'

'But she was so nice and friendly,' I replied. 'How can you say those things?'

'It's a woman's intuition,' Kate said.

'All right. We'll add her into the mix. So now we have three suspects. Next, we have to decide how to proceed with those,' concluded Alec.

Chapter Five

As we drove back to Daybreak winery, I had a strong feeling that something was not right. Kate had talked about women's intuition related to people and their behaviour. With me it was not about people so much as situations. It began with a sick feeling in the pit of my stomach. It continued with heightened awareness. Something in the air. Something sensed in the atmosphere.

'Something is terribly wrong,' I said as the car drove into the winery carpark.

Alec and Kate looked at me with questions in their eyes.

'It's a feeling. The Scottish call it "the sight." Others call it "extra-sensory perception" or "sixth sense." My family liked to think it is a Celtic trait, but I know people from other cultures also experience similar feelings from time to time.'

'What do you see?' asked Kate. Her eyes looked troubled.

'I don't know. Something is terribly wrong. There is death in the air. We will have to get out and walk around.'

Kate shivered. She felt my fear.

Alec gave me a quizzical look. He parked the car, and we climbed out. Something willed me to walk towards the vineyard.

'Come quickly,' I shouted.

Alec and his daughter came at a run. Alec was breathing heavily by the time they reached me. 'Haven't run that far so quickly in a long time,' he gasped.

He bent over and breathed deeply for a few moments.

'Tyre tracks. Single tracks from a motorbike,' I said fearfully as I pointed. Someone has been riding a motorbike around the vineyard, up and down the rows of vines.

'What is that bundle on the ground over there,' called Kate pointing to the end of a row in the vineyard some distance away.

We looked in the direction her arm was pointing, and I began running.

I dropped to my knees by the bundle. It was a body. 'Keep back,' I shouted to Kate. 'Call an ambulance and the police as fast as you can. Stay away.'

She pulled her mobile phone from her pocket and began dialling. Alec reached me and dropped to his knees too.

'Noooooooooo! Not Mark,' he cried.

I reached for Mark's neck trying to find a pulse. There was none. 'He's gone,' I said quietly. 'Look at the rope tied around his feet. Someone has dragged him around the vineyard until he died. This is a foul murder,' I added angrily. 'Someone will pay for this.'

Before long we could hear the wail of a siren. The ambulance was close. Soon it entered the gate to the vineyard. I stood and did a double arm wave. The ambulance assistant spotted me and directed the driver towards us.

The vehicle stopped, and the two officers opened the rear door and pulled a trolley from their vehicle before wheeling it to where we stood.

'He's dead boys,' I said, 'But treat him well. He is our friend.'

The ambulance driver opened his tool bag and pulled out a sharp knife to cut the rope around Mark's legs.

'Stop,' I shouted. 'The police will want evidence.' I took out my phone and took several shots of Mark's body. I moved so I could photograph the rope around his legs. As I was doing that, a police car drove through the gateway and approached us.

'Give them a few moments to view the situation,' I said to the ambulance team.

The police sergeant opened the passenger door and climbed out.

'Hullo, Alec. Hi Sean, and hi Kate,' Bob said as he slowly walked closer, frowning. 'What has happened here?'

I shook my head sadly, my face grim. 'We've just arrived home and found that Mark has been towed around the vineyard behind a motorbike. He's dead – murdered. We're totally shocked.'

The sergeant called his driver over. 'Take photos of the body, the rope, and the tyre tracks, as quick as you can, and watch where you tread. Don't walk over any tracks.'

The driver pulled out his phone and opened the camera. He hurried around taking shot after shot after shot.

The sergeant turned to Alec. 'Do you know what has caused this?'

Alec took a deep breath. His face was troubled, and tears began to gather in the corners of his eyes. 'You remember about the wrongly labelled bad wine.'

Bob nodded.

'Yesterday we found that the labels were ordered and paid for with a scammed card. A biker staying at the Clare Caravan Park ordered the mailbox and presumably collected the labels. Mark went down to the park to identify the guy and received a rough reception. There were three Harley bikers in the group. We think they might have had a hand in gluing the labels to the bad

43

wine. Now it seems they have come here and murdered Mark.'

Alec burst into tears and stumbled. Kate ran across to him to hold and console him.

Bob opened his phone and called the station. When his call was answered, he shouted, 'Mike, get a team together and hurry to the Clare Caravan Park. Arrest three bikers asap.'

He closed his phone with a snap. 'That was a stupid thing for Mark to do!' He turned to me. 'We'll send a forensics team here tomorrow. They can take plaster casts of the tyre tracks. I'll take the rope with me now.'

'All yours,' he said to the paramedic. 'Get your head doctor to examine the body and prepare a report for the coroner.'

The paramedic cut the rope from Mark's legs before he and his assistant lifted the body onto the trolley.

The sergeant bent and retrieved the rope, rolled it up, bagged it, and took it to his car. The driver finished his photo shoot and joined Bob in the car. They drove off.

The ambulance men settled Mark's body in the back of their vehicle and left. They didn't turn on the siren. Nobody needed warning that they were carrying a dead body.

We trudged our way to the Cellar Door Sales entrance. Nobody spoke. We were so distraught that tears ran down our faces. Eventually Alec found a bottle of wine and three glasses. We slumped in chairs around a central table.

'Let's drink to Mark's memory,' said Alec.

'To Mark,' I said as I raised my glass to my lips.

'To Mark,' echoed Kate before a stream of tears choked her up.

'Let's not get maudlin,' I said. 'Let's get angry. Mark's death is another part of this bloody battle being waged against you. We have a good idea where to look for who did this. We will find the culprit and we will have vengeance.'

'Amen to that,' said Alec.

Kate nodded in agreement but then another flood of tears coursed down her face. She let them run. She was too upset to find a tissue to wipe them away. I put my arm around her and held her tightly until the tears slowed down.

* * *

Mark's absence left a huge hole in our day. Routine things got done without any enthusiasm.

Forensics police arrived the next morning and took plaster casts of the motorbike tyre marks. As they left, one of them said, 'We found three different sets of tyre treads. By the way, the boss says those three bikies have disappeared. We don't know where they are so be careful.'

'We'll be careful,' Alec replied.

I sat down with my notebook and began to make notes. I recorded our impressions of the people in the seven wineries we had visited. I put big circles around the fourth, fifth and seventh entries.

'What are you up to?' asked Kate as she came back into the room.

'Just making notes about our winery visits yesterday.'

'Can I help?'

'Sure. Let's do some brainstorming about how to advance our investigations of the three we thought were dodgy,' I suggested.

'How do you want to do that?'

'I want to make a list of any ideas that come to mind. It doesn't matter how crazy. We will evaluate the list later.'

'Talk to people in the wine shops about their sales,' she suggested.

'Good one, Kate. Talk to Dave about how quickly they pay their storage fees.'

'Can we trust Dave?'

'Have to until he gives us a reason not to,' I replied.

'Talk to their cleaners,' said Kate.

'Cleaners? Why so?'

'Cleaners know everything about how an organisation is operating.'

'Yes, I guess you are right. I would like to talk to their bankers, but I'm not at all sure they would want to talk to us about their customers.'

'Perhaps we could ... Hello, Dad.'

'What mischief are you two hatching?' asked Alec.

'Helpful mischief, hopefully,' answered Kate.

'We are brainstorming ways we might be able to advance our investigations of the wineries.'

'Good. But you'll have to put that on the back burner for now. The son of your restauranteur has arrived. He wants to talk with us about the food we want him to supply.'

'Where is Angelo?' I asked.

'Checking out the kitchen facilities.'

'Let's go and meet him,' I said. 'I know his dad well, but I haven't had much to do with his son.'

I grabbed my notebook, scribbled a few words then tore the page from the book. I rose with the paper in my hand, and we walked together into the kitchen area.

'Hi, you must be Angelo,' I greeted.

'And I know you are Sean. I've seen you when you come into our restaurant on Norwood Parade. My father never stops talking about how much you helped him when he needed assistance.'

'That was a long time ago. Your father has fed me many wonderful meals since that time.'

Kate looked at me with an inquisitive look on her face that said, *there is a story here that I want you to tell me.*

I smiled at her and said, 'Another time.'

Alec took over the conversation and briefed Angelo about the Food and Wine Gourmet Week and the kinds of foods he thought would be popular. The chef needed to know approximately how many customers would want food each day. Their conversation moved on to menu choices and the kinds of wine that would suit each meal.

Angelo made notes as they talked. He checked the refrigerator capacity and said he would tow up a cool room trailer that would need to be parked close to the kitchen. Eventually, he and Alec decided they knew each other well enough to trust each other's judgement. They discussed staff numbers and money matters.

When the chef decided he knew everything he needed to know, he gathered his things. He would be back the following Friday with staff, cool room trailer and enough food to last the week.

As he stood to take his leave, I thrust my piece of paper into his hand. 'This is for your father,' I explained. 'He is checking a few things for me. Please ask him to concentrate on this list. He will know what I mean?'

Angelo looked at me, a wide smile on his face. 'He's doing some digging for you, eh? This isn't the first time from what I've heard.'

'He has amazing resources,' was all I said as I returned the smile.

He tucked the paper into a pocket as he left the room.

After he had gone, Alec turned to me. 'I have to thank you, Sean. Angelo is just the person I hoped to have organising the food. He seems thorough and knowledgeable about his business. Hope his team can do a great job.'

'You can relax,' I replied. 'He will be a real credit to your gourmet activities. The food will be outstanding, and everything will run like clockwork.'

I returned to the table in the Cellar Door Sales area to collect my papers. As I packed them into my satchel, Kate approached.

'Sean, I have something to ask,' she said quietly.

I turned to her with a smile. 'Ask away.'

'I'd like to come home with you tonight. I don't want to be alone. I want you to help me forget the last two days for a while.'

'But you have your father?'

'You know what I mean. I need to be close to you. Dad will find a bottle of Scotch and mourn in his own way. I can't help him with that.'

'I understand,' I said, 'Let your father know, then we'll be off.'

We were soon in my car heading back to my place in Armagh. I had a small vineyard where I grew Cabernet

Sauvignon that Alec was pleased to blend with his fruit because of the quality.

Kate sat quietly wrapped in her grief. I reached and touched her hand. She grasped mine tightly. A small smile struggled to escape from her lips as she whispered a faint, 'Thank you.'

When we reached my house, I escorted her to the door with one arm round her slim body. She melted into me, needing to feel loved and cared for. I needed relief from my grief too. I was pleased she was with me.

Chapter Six

The following few days were difficult for us. First, we had to attend the Coroner's Court. We took our places in the local court room where the circuit judge acted as the coroner. The court was full. Mark had been a popular winemaker in the Valley. Many of his friends wanted to know the details of his murder.

The Judge called first for the police report. The local Police Sergeant sketched out the details of Mark being tied up and dragged by a motorbike around the vineyard until he was dead.

'Do you have any leads?' asked the Judge.

'Our forensic officer found the tyre treads of three motor bikes that were involved in the murder. When a team of my officers went to the caravan park to arrest the three Harley riders, they found they had disappeared. We are searching for them now, 'explained the sergeant.

Next the Judge asked the hospital's head doctor for his report of the examination of the body.

'Your Honour, the body showed scrapes and contusions consistent with being dragged around the vineyard by the feet behind a motorbike. His head had suffered blows, which we believe could have been caused by hitting a number of trellis posts. In addition, there were bruises on his body, which we assume were caused by being kicked with steel-capped boots.'

'In your opinion, Doctor, how would you classify this murder?'

'Callous, Your Honour.'

Alec was called to the stand to describe the situation when we found the body. He broke down in tears halfway through his description and was unable to continue.

The judge scanned the court. 'Is there someone else who can complete this report.'

I stood up.

'And you are…?'

'Sean O'Connor, business consultant to Daybreak Winery and close friend of the owner, Mr Alec Marchison and the deceased.'

'Were you with the owner when the body was found?'

'Yes, Your Honour.'

'Can you please take the stand and complete the description of how the body was found.'

I took the stand and completed the events including the arrival of the ambulance and police.'

'Was Mark Brook dead when you found him?'

'Yes, Your Honour. I felt for a pulse and found none.'

'Thank you. You may return to your seat.'

The Judge banged his gavel. 'I want it recorded that Mark Brook was callously murdered by person or persons unknown. I urge the Police to do their utmost to find the murderer or murderers as quickly as possible. The court proceedings are now complete. I wish to thank all who have attended and shown their support for the deceased.'

He banged his gavel again, rose from his desk and disappeared through a curtain into the rooms at the rear of the courthouse.

We rose but found it difficult to move very far towards the court doorway. Many of the people wanted to tender their condolences and offer Alec support. Tears still streamed down his face, and he was almost unable to speak. I put my arm through one of his and Kate did the same on his other side. Tears ran freely down her face as well, but she did her best to copy my lead and help me slowly move Alec through the crowd. We nodded and answered the well-meaning comments and platitudes as best we could while slowly steering Alec towards the door.

We arranged the funeral for two days later. Mark had no partner. Alec had details of his parents who lived in Port Pirie, so he contacted them and offered them accommodation. They drove into town late the next day and I met them and showed them to their accommodation.

True to tradition, a light misty shower set the tone for the funeral. The church was packed by well-wishers and supporters, and the priest gave a very complimentary description of Mark's life and his character. Heads nodded in agreement all around the pews. Mark was one of those people who would go out of his way to help those in need.

We moved from the church to the graveyard. After that, everyone was invited back to Daybreak Winery for a wake. Most came, had the obligatory glass or two of wine then drifted home.

'Did you see any of our suspects at the funeral?' I asked after the last person had left.

Alec shook his head. 'I didn't see Kurt, Nigel, or Cynthia. Did you see them?

'I don't know Nigel or Kurt,' I replied, 'but I didn't see Cynthia.'

'Kate?'

'I've met Nigel before, but I didn't see him or Cynthia.'

'So, we still have three suspects,' I said.

'Three suspects who may have links to a murderer and who may have planned a foul trick on our wines. Who do we know that can organise the buying of our labels with a stolen credit card, attach them to bad wine and then organise to murder our winemaker?'

'It beggars' belief,' I said.

'Come on, Sean,' teased Kate. 'You are the super sleuth. How do we solve this mystery?'

'By doing some hard sleuthing,' I replied. I tried to find a grin, but my emotional drain had dried up my grins. 'I am at a loss at the moment, but something will break soon. It always does,' I said with as much positivity as I could muster.

* * *

The next day, Alec decided to do an inventory of the wine he had at the winery that could be sold during the Food and Wine Gourmet event. It was not something I wanted to help him with, and to be honest, I thought he needed to do something absorbing to take his mind off Mark's murder.

'Kate,' I said. 'How about we have lunch at Skillogalee Winery? They have delicious food and some good wines too. I love the old stone settlers' cottage. Its ambiance is great.'

'Sounds good to me,' she answered.

Before long we were driving from Clare to Sevenhill. We chatted about the scenery and Kate's study, keeping very carefully away from Mark's murder and the fake wine business. We needed to take a break from the heavy stuff that dominated our lives, even though it was there just under the surface, threatening to break out at any moment.

At Sevenhill, we turned right and headed into the hills. Before long we were entering Skillogalee from Trevarrick Road. The vineyards spread around the hill's face, leading us to the old stone cottage that had been built in 1853. It had been turned into a treasure by the current owners.

We walked into the shop to explore the wines displayed on wooden shelves and read some of the awards festooning the wall. Then we found a table on the front verandah that gave us spectacular views of the manicured gardens, shady trees, and vineyards.

We spent some time drooling over the menu.

'I don't know what to choose,' said Kate. 'Everything looks scrumptious.'

'You can come back again so close your eyes, rotate your finger and point.'

She laughed, eventually selecting the Market Fish with Chardonnay to drink. I chose the Steak Frites with a glass of Cabernet. Once our orders were placed, we settled down to a relaxing afternoon.

Our food arrived and we tucked into a delicious meal and sipped well-crafted wine.

Kate hadn't been here before, so she was looking around, admiring the nooks and crannies. Suddenly she grabbed my arm. 'Look,' she said. 'Motorbikes behind those trees.'

I followed her gaze. Three Harleys. My stomach muscles tightened. *Does one have a tow ball,* I wondered?

'We've finished our food. I'll go and pay then we can take a pleasant stroll through the garden,' I suggested.

'Yes,' she said. Her tone showed her interest was piqued.

She's a goer, this girl, I thought. *Ready for anything. She's a keeper.*

We meandered, looking at trees and shrubs, commenting on flowers. Just a guy and his girl enjoying each other and the environment.

We came close enough to the Harleys to notice that one had a tow ball for a small trailer. Then I stared in shock. *No. I don't believe it.* The owner had left his keys in the ignition. My mind started leaping.

'Kate. I'm sure that bike belongs to Racoon. I think he killed Mark. I'm going to borrow that bike and take it to the police. They need to check it for rope burn and take impressions of the tyres. If I don't, the bikies will disappear again, and we will have no evidence.'

She looked at me. 'You're not serious, are you? You are!' she decided. 'Check with the police first. I don't want you arrested for theft of a motorbike.'

'You're right. I'll give them a call.'

I called Sergeant Bob Murray at the Clare police station. 'Bob, I'm at Skillogalee Winery and I've found the Harley that I think might be the one used to kill Mark. It has the keys in it so I'm thinking of bringing it in to you to check. Are you okay with that?'

'Yes, Sean. Borrowing, I presume, not stealing.'

'Exactly. I should be there in not much more than ten minutes. Can you please have someone on the front gate to have it open for me? Instruct them to shut it tight as soon as I am in. Can you please also have someone at the shed at the rear of the police station with the door open? I'll be coming in fast with some angry bikers close behind.'

'Okay, Sean. We'll be ready. Don't take any risks.'

'Joke of the week,' I replied as I closed the call.

'How do I help?' asked Kate.

'Let's take a quick walk around to find where those bikers are.'

We walked through a group of ornamental gums and spotted the three guys a short distance away.

'As soon as I start up the bike they will come running. I want you to take the car and follow me, but slowly so you block their path. At the gate turn right.'

'Turn right? But that's not the way to Clare.'

'I will be turning left, and I want them to chase me. As soon as those guys come after me, I want you to drive back and collect their wine glasses. Hold them only by the stem so your fingerprints don't mingle with theirs. Put the glasses in plastic shopping bags. You will find some in the car behind the driver's seat. Then follow me to Clare, but don't get too close.'

'Where will I find you?'

'Wait for me in the Middle Pub. Ready, Kate?'

'Ready, Sean,' she replied. Anxiety was written all over her face. She took the car keys from me and walked quickly to my car. I walked with her to retrieve my leather coat from the back seat.

'A quick kiss for luck,' I suggested.

She gave me a quick peck on the cheek. 'You just take care,' she said. 'I don't want you dead too.'

I could see she was putting on a brave face, but she was even more apprehensive of the outcome of this crazy venture than I was. I tried to reassure her. 'I have no intention of leaving this planet just yet.' I could see by her frown that I had failed miserably.

Back at the bike, I borrowed the helmet that had been left on the seat, lifted a leg over the saddle and turned the key. The engine caught quickly with a loud roar. I lifted the gear lever with my left foot to engage first gear and took off, raising a cloud of dust and small pebbles.

I heard yells behind me from the bikers but took no notice. I opened the throttle and did a crazy tap dance on the gear lever as I advanced through the gears. I was doing almost a hundred clicks an hour by the time I reached the gate. I braked, spread my left knee to give me wind to pull the bike around to the left, and away I went like the clappers of hell.

As I turned to the right on the next bend, I glanced back and saw my car driven by Kate blocking the gateway. *That should slow them down a little*, I hoped.

Before long I turned onto the main road to Clare. A little way along I saw a car pulling a caravan begin to turn into the main road ahead of me. I flattened the bike, did a crazy zig zag around the car and caravan, almost taking some of their paint with me. I just managed to swing back into the left lane as a car came at me from the other direction. I caught a glimpse of an angry face and a shaking fist as I left the caravan behind me. I hoped it would slow down my pursuers.

I raced the bike along the highway, going way over the speed limit when I could. I left behind a sea of angry drivers, shaking heads and fists and no doubt hurling loud obscenities at my retreating back. It was a dangerous and crazy but fast trip. I didn't slow down until I entered the main street of Clare. I breathed a sigh of relief when I saw a police officer holding the main gate to the police station open for me.

I hurtled through and heard the clang as the gate was shut behind me. The shed door was open. I whizzed in and came to a screeching halt. Another police officer lowered the lift-up door and let me out of the shed through a side door. I walked quickly into the office, stripping off my leather coat and helmet as I did so.

'You made it in one piece, I see,' said Bob. 'I'll have the bike checked for rope burn marks.'

'Don't forget to check the tyre treads for a match to your plaster casts,' I added.

'Of course. And fingerprints from the bike to see if he is a known criminal.'

'You will have some more fingerprints to check when Kate brings in their wine glasses. You can also check on the two others he travels with.'

60

'Boy, you have been busy. Let's hope we can nail Mark's murderer.'

'That's what I have risked my life for, Bob. Can you please store this leather jacket for me for a couple of days? I don't want our biker friends to see me with it just now.'

'Okay, Sean. I'll do that for you.'

'Kate should now be over at the Middle Pub. She'll bring the wine glasses over in a while.'

'Excellent. Go and have a stiff drink. I'd say your system needs some calming down after that ride.'

I smiled as I left his office. As I was about to cross the road, I heard the thunder of two Harleys coming slowly down the main street. I turned and appeared to gaze with rapt attention at a pair of cowboy boots in a shop display. In reality, I was watching their reflections in the window, one bike with one rider and the other bike with my adversary riding pillion. Their gaze swept from side to side. When they had passed, I crossed the street and stepped into the Middle Pub.

Several drinkers sat on tall stools near the bar. Kate sat at a side table with two drinks, a glass of wine for her and a stiff scotch for me. As soon as she saw me, she jumped up and ran into my open arms. 'Don't you ever do that to me again.' Her smile turned from scolding to a hungry loving look that could have devoured me. 'I love you, Sean. Too much to see you die.'

'Luck was with me this time,' I said and gave her a big kiss.

Loud claps and comments echoed around the bar.

'Don't ever do it again, mate, whatever it was,' said one beery voice.

His comment prompted laughter from the other drinkers.

We sat talking, letting our adrenalin levels drop back to somewhere near normal. Eventually, we decided it was time to head home. The bikers had disappeared, so we took the wine glasses to the police station before heading back to the winery.

Chapter Seven

The next morning, Sergeant Bob Murray called Alec. 'Could you and Sean come into the station as soon as possible.'

'What's the hurry, Bob,' queried Alec.

'I have some puzzling results from the Harley Sean brought in. I need to discuss them with you asap. Today would be great if you can manage it.'

'We'll be in straight after lunch. Will that work for you?'

'That's fine, Alec. See you then.'

Alec closed the call, rose from his office chair, and came in search of me. He found me puzzling over more notes I had made of the winery visits.

'Making any progress?' asked Alec.

'Not yet. Just a few ideas to explore.'

'Bob wants us at the police station after lunch. He said he wants to talk about the results from the bike.'

* * *

After lunch, we drove into Clare and pulled up near the police station.

'Come into my office,' invited Bob when we entered the police station.

He ushered us into seats in his office and closed the door.

'Thank you for coming in promptly,' he began. 'I'm afraid we have a problem. The bike you brought in, Sean, was not involved in Mark's murder.'

I almost fell out of the chair in shock. 'Not the bike?'

'No. We found no rope burn marks, and the tyre treads did not match the plaster moulds we took at the winery. This was not the bike that killed Mark. Your angry biker from the Caravan Park was not the murderer.'

Alec and I sat in total shock.

'I could charge you with stealing a bike, Sean, but I know your intentions were for the best reason. However, I have to warn you not to go off half-cocked again without substantial evidence.'

I nodded. I felt angry that I had not discovered the murderer and embarrassed at making a fool of myself in front of the law. *Stupid, stupid, stupid,* I told myself and gave myself a mental slap on the wrist.

'Sorry, Bob,' I said slowly. 'I was sure I had our man, but I was wrong. I apologise sincerely. What will you do about the bike?'

'We've had a call from the caravan park manager to say our villains are back there today. I'll send an officer down to tell the owner his bike has been found and he can collect it from the police station.'

'But what about the Post Office mailbox and the receiving of Alec's labels. Can we pin that on him?'

'Maybe, but I would need an identification from the Post Office lady, and at the moment I'm not sure how to arrange that.'

'What about photographing the guy when he comes to claim his bike?'

Bob thought for a moment or two. 'I can get an identity from the bike's registration, but it may be false. I need you, Alec, to officially report the fraudulent ordering and receiving of your stolen labels. He must have handled them at some stage so we might be able to match the fingerprints on the bottle labels with his prints from the bike and wine glasses Kate brought in. If we can do that, then we can arrest him.'

'I'll report that immediately,' said Alec. 'You make up the words, Bob, and I'll sign it. Anything to further the investigation. There must have been others in on this scam, but at least this makes a start.'

I brightened up a little. A tiny ray of sunshine was beginning to shine through the cracks. But we needed more help.

A police officer knocked on Bob's office door.

'Come,' said Bob.

A head poked around the door. 'Serg, I found something you might like to know about.'

'What is it, Adam?' asked Bob with a frown. He didn't want to be interrupted at this moment.

'I was doing a final check of the Harley when I found a post office mailbox key in one of the panier bags.'

Bob leapt from his office chair in excitement. 'Show me, quickly.'

Adam handed over the key in a clear evidence bag. Bob turned the bag over to read the number on the tag.

'271,' he shouted and did a little dance. 'You little beauty! Hurry with this to the fingerprint guy. Get him to check to see if the prints match our Harley mate.'

Adam retrieved the bag and hurried out the door.

The tiny ray of sunshine was growing stronger and wider.

Bob and Alec together quickly drafted a crime report about the fraudulent purchase of the labels and how they were attached to non-Daybreak wine. Alec signed the report and Bob asked his forensic guy to check the fingerprints taken from the box of inferior wine for a match with fingerprints on the bike, the mailbox key and the wine glasses Kate had brought in.

Bob and Alec chatted for a while about the coming Food and Wine Gourmet Week while I let my mind run around the pieces of evidence we had so far.

An hour later, the forensic guy came back into the office with a huge smile on his face. 'Serg. We've found matches. The three motor bike riders' fingerprints are on the labels. That means the three of them took part in gluing the labels onto bottles of substandard wine. The leader's fingerprints are also on the post office mailbox key.'

'At last, a breakthrough,' said the sergeant with a grin as he jumped up from his chair. He poked his head through the door and called out, 'Mike, take a team of six officers and the paddy wagon. Arrest the three bikers at the Caravan Park. They'll give you trouble so be prepared for a bit of rough stuff. I don't mind how rough you have to get, but you didn't hear me say that.'

Bob came back into the office, bouncing with energy. 'Finally, we have some concrete evidence so, Sean, perhaps it was good fortune that you were at Skillogalee yesterday. The stolen bike was finally useful to us, but Kate 'borrowing' the wine glasses was a stroke of pure genius. Please tell her how pleased we are that she thought to bring them in.'

I smiled a small smile to myself. *She deserves some praise for her courage*, I thought.

My phone rang.

'Sean speaking.'

'Hi, Mate. It's Ken. Mandy and I decided to come up a couple of days early. Are you still okay with that bed?'

'Of course. Glad to have you. You are just in time to help us solve a crime or two. And we now have a murder for you as well. Where are you?'

'We've just entered Clare.'

'Park outside the Police Station. I'll meet you.'

'Great. On our way.'

I turned to the others. 'My mate Detective Inspector Ken Harris has just arrived in Clare. I invited him and his wife, Mandy, to stay with me and enjoy the Food and Wine Gourmet activities. He's come a couple of days early so he might like to help us with our problems. Are you okay with that, Bob?'

'More the merrier, Sean. He's a great detective so I'm happy for him to take over if he wants to do that.'

'I don't know that he would want to, but his experience will be helpful. You okay with that, Alec?'

'Certainly. Just in time, I'd say. His assistance should be worth heaps.'

'I'll take them home now and show them the house. How about I ask him to join us here tomorrow morning. Is that okay?'

'Fine with me,' said Bob.

'Excellent timing,' said Alec. 'Bring them both around to the winery for dinner tonight, Sean. Kate can show Mandy around tomorrow while we come here.'

'Sounds good,' I said as I walked from the office.

I reached the street just as Ken parked opposite the police station. I waved a welcome then pointed to my car parked a little further up the street. Ken nodded and waited for me to pull out of the park before following. A little later, we pulled up alongside my house, and I helped them with their baggage.

'Nice quiet place you have here,' said Mandy.

'Just me and the magpies, and occasionally some deer passing through,' I answered with a smile.

I showed them the bedroom and gave them time to unpack as I made a pot of coffee.

'Alec has invited us to dinner at the winery tonight,' I told them as I poured a cup each.

'That's very nice,' said Mandy. 'Should we take anything? A salad or a dessert perhaps?'

'No, Mandy. Alec won't expect that on your first night in the Valley. But I suggest we invite him and Kate here for dinner another night. I know you are a chef extraordinaire so I will leave that in your hands.'

'Who's Kate?' she asked. 'His wife?'

'No, his daughter who is studying law. His wife passed away a few years ago.'

'That's sad,' she empathised.

'Alright, young man,' said Ken. 'What's going on with your stolen wine labels, and did you mention a murder?'

'We've nailed the guy who organised the mailbox and presumably collected the labels. He and his two biker mates glued those labels to the crap wine. Some other Harley riders murdered Alec's winemaker. We still have a long way to go in finding the murderers and solving the rest of the crime. You are invited to the police station tomorrow morning to be briefed. Mandy, Kate will take you around and introduce you to the Valley. Hope that is okay with you both.'

'Wouldn't have it any other way,' answered Ken. 'I was sure you would dream up something to prevent me from dying from boredom.'

'I look forward to being shown around,' said Mandy. 'Is Kate a nice person, Sean?'

'She's the best. She's a lovely person. You will get on very well with her.'

Mandy looked at me with interest. Something in my tone must have given the game away.

'Oh, it's like that, is it?' she asked, a broad smile crossing her face.

I nodded and I'm ashamed to say a slight blush coloured my face.

'Now,' I said briskly. 'Bring your cups and I'll show you around my country abode.'

We walked around the vineyard, garden, and sheds for a while, then returned to the house to freshen up for dinner.

Before long we set off for the winery. Alec met us at the door, and I introduced my guests. Kate walked swiftly from the kitchen straight to me for a kiss and cuddle. I introduced her to my guests.

She noticed Mandy smiling. 'You told her,' she whispered.

'No, she guessed,' I said with a smile. 'She's looking forward to being taken around the Valley by you tomorrow. She's a delightful lady. You'll get on well.'

'I know we will,' she answered. 'Any friend of yours is a friend of mine.'

'Come on you two. Time for dinner,' reminded Alec.

Chapter Eight

The following morning, I drove Ken and Mandy to the winery. Kate met us in the carpark. She gave me a good morning hug and kiss before taking Mandy's arm.

'Are you ready for your guided tour of the Valley, Madam?'

'Don't be so formal. I'm happy to have you show me around. I'm looking forward to it,' she said with a smile. 'We'll have more fun than the boys. I'm also looking forward to hearing more about this relationship between you and Sean. He has been our friend for a long time and has needed someone like you in his life.'

Kate smiled before escorting her to the car.

I watched somewhat ruefully. I knew they would have a more enjoyable day than we would. Alec came out and joined me and Ken in my car.

'Morning, Ken,' he said. 'Morning, Sean. I'm looking forward to some real progress in our investigation.'

We soon pulled up outside the police station. Bob was waiting for us when we entered the office. 'Our boys aren't talking at the moment. Do you want to interview them, Ken?' he asked.

'Too soon,' Ken answered. 'Let them sweat on it for a while. We need to go over the details of the case. Can we use your office, Bob?'

'Certainly. Come this way.'

We moved into Bob's office and closed the door. Bob offered Ken his chair behind the desk, but Ken shook his head sideways. 'This is your case,' he said. 'I'm just here to lend a hand.'

Bob and I both knew that it wouldn't be long before Ken took over, but we let him pretend he was only helping.

'I would like you to fill me in this morning. Alec, could you begin from the start of this awful business?'

Alec described finding the poor-quality wine with his label on the bottle and finding a pallet of the crap wine with his label attached in the wine store. 'I believe you know that Sean approached the label printers and found they had been ordered by phone and paid for with a scammed credit card.'

Ken nodded. 'I know about the mailbox where the labels were delivered, and I believe you have been able to apprehend the persons who helped attach them to the bottles of poor-quality wine. Let's get to the murder of your winemaker. What did he do to cause that?'

Alec described how Mark had approached the bikers in the Clare Caravan Park and their response.

'So, we now know that the biker who organised the mailbox and presumably collected the labels was not the murderer. But he was obviously in touch with someone who was pulling the strings. Why did three others on Harleys come to the winery to murder Mark? Where did they come from? And the big question, who paid these guys to carry out the wine bottle switching and the murder? Someone with a lot of money wants to destroy your business, Alec, so you can't win any more wine competitions. It seems this person is prepared to hire thugs to carry out a deception and a murder.'

'That's it in a nutshell.' I said admiringly.

'I haven't finished,' said Ken in an irritated voice.

'Sorry,' I offered.

'If you are not to win the wine competition, Alec, who wants the crown?' Ken continued. 'Let's look at the big picture here. Someone with lots of money and the ability to hire thugs, wants another winery to win the competition badly enough to hatch a complicated plan to put you out of the running. Does this sound like someone you know in the Clare Valley?'

We both shook our heads sideways.

'My guess is that this complicated plan has been devised and carried out by someone from outside the valley. We don't know why. We also don't know which local winery is in cahoots with the money figure. Someone in the Valley has agreed to or been pressured to play a central part in this scam. Your thoughts?'

Alec spoke up. 'I approached the wine judges and discovered there are eight wineries entering their wines in the Cabernet Sauvignon section of the competition. That means seven other wineries could be involved.'

'That narrows the field,' said Ken. 'What do we know about them?'

Alec described how we went on a tour of those wineries and decided three of them could be our enemy.

'Tell me about those three. Why have you come to that conclusion?'

Alec described our winery trip and the responses to our visit from the three we had chosen.

Ken listened carefully and made notes in a notebook.

'Bob. What are your staff numbers?'

Bob looked at Ken in surprise. He thought for a moment or two and said, 'I have 9 bodies on my staff normally, but we will have another 20 joining us from Port Pirie for the duration of the Food and Wine Gourmet week. Some will patrol the roads, and some will show their presence at the wineries to watch for those who drink more wine than they can handle.'

'Good,' said Ken.

Bob waited for a reason for the question, but Ken said no more on that subject.

'Do you have a program for the week's activities?'

'Yes,' replied Bob. 'Would you like me to get you a copy now.'

'Later, thanks.'

face. 'Now give me another kiss and cuddle. I need to feel you in my arms.'

She came to me with a wide smile, 'You are impossible, but I suppose I can put up with that.'

Chapter Nine

Next morning a fancy car drove up the main street of Clare and parked near the police station. A portly, middle-aged man in an expensive suit climbed from the car and entered the front office.

'How can I help, Sir?' asked the young policewoman on the front desk.'

'I want to see the person in charge,' he said commandingly.

'That would be Sergeant Bob Murray,' she said politely. 'I'll see if he is available.'

'He'd better be.'

She walked into Bob's office and said, 'A very rude man wants to see you now.'

Bob smiled at her. 'We'll let him stew for a few moments. Go back and tell him I'll be there in a little while.'

She smiled as she turned to the door.

'The Sergeant is very busy. He'll be with you in a little while,' she said politely then turned to her computer screen.

The man fumed and paced up and down the room, obviously very annoyed to get the brush off.

Eventually, Bob came from his office. 'You wanted to see me?' he said in an enquiring manner.

'I object to being made to wait. I'm not an ordinary member of the public,' he almost shouted.

'Is that so?' said Bob. 'May I know who you are?'

'Aloysius Webber. I'm one of Sydney's top lawyers and I'm not used to being kept waiting.'

'What is your business?'

'I'm here to represent the men you have in jail. I demand to see them immediately.'

'Oh, is that so? Our prisoners have not asked to be represented by a lawyer,' said Bob.

'Whether they have asked or not is irrelevant. I demand to see them immediately.'

'That will not be possible. They are accessories to murder and are currently helping us with our enquiries. They are not permitted visitors.'

'But I'm here to represent them. Are you dumb or something? Don't you understand the law?'

'I understand that if they have not asked to be represented, they don't have a lawyer until we appoint one. And I can tell you it won't be someone as rude as you. Now leave the station before I charge you with being a public nuisance.'

The young policewoman ducked her head down out of sight behind her computer screen. She struggled with the urge to burst into loud laughter and tried to smother it by holding her breath.

Webber's face grew red. His blood pressure threatened to blow out the top of his head.

'How dare you! How much bail has been set?'

'None yet. That is the job of the magistrate.'

'Where do I find him?'

'In the courthouse.' Bob turned and returned to his office.

The lawyer saw he would get no further cooperation from the sergeant. He turned to the young policewoman. 'Where is the courthouse?'

'Down the street,' she answered shortly and swiftly left the office before her laughter lifted the ceiling off the building. She waved a burly policeman to take her place in the front office to make sure the objectionable lawyer left.

Webber fumed as he walked down the steps to the street. He looked around and eventually saw a Courthouse sign. He entered and asked for the magistrate. A guard at the entrance pointed to a door further down the passage. The lawyer walked to the door and knocked.

'Enter,' said a deep voice.

He entered and walked over to the magistrate's desk.

'You are ...?'

'Aloysius Webber. I'm a lawyer from Sydney.'

'Your business?'

'I'm here to pay the bail for the prisoners being kept at the police station and take them with me.'

'Oh, are you?' said the magistrate. 'Bail hasn't been set.'

'Then perhaps you can set it now and I'll pay it immediately.'

'That won't be done at your command. These prisoners are material witnesses in the brutal murder of one of our winemakers. Bail will not be set, and they will not be released on bail to anyone.'

The lawyer stood for a moment attempting to change his snarl into a smile. The magistrate watched with interest, knowing what to expect.

'How would you like a fully funded trip to the south of France? We will provide an attractive companion to keep you company.'

'I don't think my wife would like that too much,' he said, a small smile creasing his lips.

'We could provide a companion for her too.'

'Stop right now! I am not a person who accepts bribes. We don't believe in doing business that way in this hick town, which is how I believe you described us.'

The lawyer looked up in surprise. 'How do you know that?' then it clicked. 'Someone told you I was coming. Who was it?'

'That's for me to know and you to guess,' said the magistrate. 'Who sent you here?'

'No one you need to know about.'

'Go back to Sydney where you belong,' the magistrate said firmly, 'We don't believe in being dishonest and deceitful. We believe in honesty and fair dealing. Leave now before I report you to the police for trying to bribe me.'

The lawyer turned and stormed out the door, ignored the farewell from the guard and went straight to his car. The vehicle burned leather as it took off heading south, back to the Adelaide airport. He knew his backer would not be pleased with his inability to bring the prisoners with him.

Ken, Alec, and I arrived at the police station as the lawyer took off in his fancy car.

'We were nearly bowled over by a car leaving town in a hurry,' I said to Bob when we entered his office.

'That was the fancy lawyer you told us about. He didn't get the cooperation he expected. He was rude and abrasive.'

'Not only that,' said the magistrate who entered Bob's office just behind us.

We turned and looked at the magistrate with interest. 'He tried to bribe me with an all-expenses paid holiday to the south of France with an attractive companion to keep me company. Would you believe that?'

'He must be bankrolled by big money in Sydney,' remarked Ken. 'Why would big money be interested in the Clare Valley? What is the motivation for destroying one winery by setting up a fake wine scam and murdering the chief winemaker? Obviously, another winery is involved, but why?'

We all shared the concerns but at that moment had no answers.

A knock sounded on Bob's door. 'Come,' he called.

A junior officer poked his head in the door and said, 'The contingent from Port Pirie has arrived.'

We could hear chattering in the outer office.

'Take them into the main meeting room,' Bob ordered, 'and find those maps and Gourmet programs for our newcomers. Gentlemen, would you like to meet our additional staff members?'

Bob shepherded us into a large meeting room. We took seats near the front of the room.

'Ladies and gentlemen. Thank you all for swelling our numbers for next week. As you leave the room, you will each receive a map of the valley and a Food and Wine Gourmet program, as well as information about your accommodation and job rosters for the week.

'In a little while, I will explain your duties and the attitude I expect you to adopt during the Gourmet Week, but first I would like to introduce you to Detective Inspector Ken Harris from the Adelaide Crime

Investigation Branch who is leading an investigation into several serious local crimes.'

The newly arrived police officers looked in interest as Ken stood up to address the group. He outlined the crimes of fake wine and the murder of a winemaker.

'I want you to be on the watch for anyone who might be linked to these crimes. We have in custody the men who helped attach the labels to wine bottles containing inferior product. They ride Harleys and at first, we thought they were the riders who attacked a winemaker and dragged him around his vineyard behind a bike until he was dead. Unfortunately, their bikes tyres didn't match the tracks in the vineyard. So, we are looking for another three Harley riders who might have committed the murder.'

'Sir, can I speak,' asked one of the Port Pirie policemen.

'Permission granted,' said Ken.

'On our way from Pirie this morning we were passed by three Harley riders coming to Clare.'

'Tell us more,' asked Ken.

We held our breath. *Is this the breakthrough we have been waiting for*, I wondered?

'These riders are well known to us as hell raisers. They are always in trouble, but we can't pin anything serious on them. They are slippery and have a good lawyer when we get them before the magistrate. They are fined from time to time, but money is no object to them.

'They seem to be rolling in the stuff, probably from drugs, but we haven't yet been able to get enough evidence. The leader calls himself Bandit.'

'We'll check if they turned up at the caravan park. If we can find them, maybe we can get impressions from their bike tyres,' Bob said.

The room went quiet, then a small female voice spoke up. 'Please, Sir, may I speak?'

'Of course,' replied Ken.

'Last night there was heavy rain and after those bikes passed us, they left the road to ride in the mud as they passed a car on the wrong side,' explained the policewoman. 'It is possible that there may still be some fresh tyre tracks in that mud.'

Excitement passed around the group. Bob jumped to his feet. 'Could you go with our forensics team to show them where that happened?'

'Yes, Sir,' she said excitedly.

'I'm Sergeant to you, not Sir. You only use Sir for the Detective Inspector, but your information might be just the breakthrough we need. Come with me now and I will introduce you to the forensics team.'

She jumped to her feet excitedly and followed Bob from the room.

'That's good policing,' said Ken to the group. 'That's what we would like from you all. Now file out. Take your information and accommodation sheets and your roster for next week.

'Spend the afternoon studying the material and taking a look around. If you have any questions, refer them to Sergeant Bob Murray. Dismissed.'

Chapter Ten

The next morning Bob rang Alec. 'We have a match of the tyre treads with the tyre impressions we took at the vineyard. We have found your murderers.'

'That's fantastic news,' replied Alec.

'We'll have them in jail shortly. I thought Sean might like the pleasure of riding the real murderer's bike in for us as we confiscate all of their bikes from the Caravan Park.'

Alec laughed. 'I'm sure he would love to do that.'

'Tell him from me it won't be quite as dangerous as the last mad ride he made.'

'I'll get Kate to take him down. He should be there soon. Bye, Bob.'

'Bye, Alec. Our luck is improving, thank goodness. We should soon have this mess sorted.'

Alec chuckled as he came to find me. He found me helping Kate assemble some new shelving in the lounge.

'Good news. The police had a positive identification of the murderer's bikes. They've gone to the Caravan Park to arrest them. Bob thought you might like to ride the real murderer's bike to the police station.'

'No, that wouldn't be exciting enough,' I said with a grin.

'Of course you will,' said Kate. Your leather jacket is still in the car. I'll drive you down now.'

We were soon in the car and on our way. When we reached the caravan park, we spotted two paddy wagons and several policemen. By the sounds of shouting and banging coming from the paddy wagons, we guessed the arrests had already been made.

I left the vehicle, wrapping my leather coat around me as I walked. One of the local policemen approached me with a bunch of keys. 'You get Bandit's bike, that black one at the front,' he said.

'What about the other bikes?' I asked.

'Some of our guys are licensed to ride so you'll have company,' he answered with a broad grin. 'Won't be as exciting as your last ride. We've all heard about that one. You were lucky not to be booked for dangerous riding and speeding, but we knew what was happening, so we looked the other way.'

'Glad you did,' I answered. 'Thanks.'

'All in a good cause, we thought.'

I pulled on a helmet and mounted the black bike. Policemen mounted the other five.

'You lead,' shouted one of the others.

I held up my thumb to signal agreement and let out the clutch.

The noise from these six machines sounded like a Harley convention. We left the park and rode sedately down the main road to Clare Police station. One guy edged up beside me and in the rear-view mirror I saw the others pairing up. Two by two, we rode at a sedate pace, the exhaust noise making everyone along the way turn and watch. No doubt it was an impressive sight. I hadn't ridden in a club event for years, so it was fun. I edged up the speed a little and all the other bikes kept with me.

As we entered the main street of Clare, cars pulled over to let us pass. They hadn't seen anything like this for a long time. The laws against biker clubs had removed much of the fun stuff. We eventually pulled up in front of the station and parked our bikes. They would all be forensically checked.

Kate wasn't far behind, so she was ready for me when I handed in the keys and helmet. 'Enjoy that, Big Boy?' she asked with a wide grin.

'Fantastic,' I replied. 'Next time, it will be on *my* bike, and you will be riding with me.'

'I look forward to it. Can't come soon enough,' she answered, a wide grin spreading across her face.

* * *

Bob called Alec a day or two later. 'You'll never believe it, but that mongrel lawyer is back again. This time he says he has a court order to give him the right to pay bail and take our prisoners away. Can you get Ken here in a hurry?'

'Sure thing, Bob. We're on our way.'

Alec ran into the dining room where we were just about to begin eating our lunch. It had been prepared by our Italian chefs. Enticing aromas filled the air.

'Bad timing. We'll have to skip lunch. The Sydney lawyer is back with a court order to allow him to see the prisoners, pay bail and escape with them back to Sydney.'

'Over my dead body!' snorted Ken. 'We'd better get down there and stop this rubbish tout suite.'

I rose to my feet, grabbing a piece of pizza as I did so.

Kate copied my move. 'I'm coming too.'

We walked swiftly to Alec's car and were soon on our way. As we entered the police station, we saw several police officers standing in a close line preventing the lawyer from pushing his way through the rear door to the cells.

The lawyer was shouting and waving his court order in the air. 'Get out of my way. I have a court order giving me permission to see the prisoners and pay their bail.'

Bob stood to one side, a grim look on his face. 'Bail will not be set for these murderers,' he shouted, trying to over-shout the lawyer.

'Shut up, the lot of you.'

I had never before heard Ken raise his voice. He was usually very calm, but I saw immediately his Irish was up and he wasn't about to bow down to anyone.

'See this court order. It gives me full rights to see the prisoners, pay their bail and take them with me,' said the lawyer commandingly.

'Let me see this court order,' commanded Ken.

The lawyer waved it in Ken's direction but kept a tight hold on the paper.

'Give it to me,' commanded Ken in a very firm voice.

'I don't need to,' argued the lawyer. 'I've already told you what it says.'

'We will not proceed until I can verify that it is what you say it is.'

'You don't trust me, one of Sydney's top lawyers?'

'NO!'

The lawyer's face fell in complete amazement. He was not used to being treated this way.

We stood behind Ken holding our breath as we watched this most unusual confrontation.

The lawyer had obviously never crossed swords with someone as strong-willed as Ken. Eventually he gave in and handed the document to Ken ungraciously. Ken took his time, reading the document from top to bottom, slowly and carefully. Then he turned to Kate. 'You are studying law,' he said. 'What have you learned about the law of jurisprudence?'

'We studied that last Semester.'

'Does a local court in New South Wales have the right to force a South Australian court to set bail for a prisoner who has offended in this state.'

'Not if the local authorities believe there is (a) an unacceptable risk of the prisoner offending again, or (b) if the authorities believe the prisoner will not attend court when required.'

I was stunned by her level of knowledge. There was so much more to be learned about this young woman. I silently made clapping motions to her.

She smiled in appreciation.

The Sydney lawyer's face grew red with increasing anger. His blood pressure was climbing steadily.

Ken nodded. 'Good answer, Kate. That solves the bail question. There won't be any. Now the other jurisprudence question relates to the power of an NSW local court to order South Australian police to give a Sydney lawyer access to prisoners.'

'My study leads me to believe that access to prisoners cannot be given to outside people while the prisoners are still 'helping' the police with their enquiries. I believe an NSW Local Court has no jurisdiction to command this access.'

'My thoughts exactly.'

He turned to the lawyer. 'How come you have the stupidity to come to this hick town, as you call it, expecting to bail these criminals and take them to Sydney so they can get lost? We are confident they will offend again, and we are quite sure they will never return to face trial.'

'How do you know so much about my private conversations? You must have spies working for you.'

'We need them with dishonest lawyers like you trying to pull the wool over our eyes. How much did you pay to have this document drawn up? It isn't worth the cost of the paper it is written on. How big was your bribe? I understand you attempted to bribe our local magistrate. If you are not out of this building in ten seconds, I will charge you with an attempt to bribe a public officer of the law in South Australia. Your keepers in Sydney will not be able to help you here.'

'But, but, but...' murmured the lawyer.

Ken folded the court document and tore it into small pieces before tossing them at the lawyer. He began to count, 'One... two... three...'

We laughed as the lawyer turned and hurried from the room. We soon heard his car start up and speed away. The police officers joined us in clapping Ken's masterly treatment of the obnoxious lawyer.

Chapter Eleven

The next morning, I decided to approach the three winery owners we judged could be guilty. 'Come on, Kate,' I called. 'We are going clue hunting.'

'Where, Sean?' was her sensible response.

'Let's go to the three wineries we suspect. We might find something useful.'

'Better than sitting here moping,' she commented. 'But don't you think there will be more danger if we stir the pot?'

'The bikers are all in jail so they can't hurt us.'

'True. Okay. Let's go.'

We climbed into my four-wheel drive and set off.

'We'll start with the Lone Dog Winery. Nigel's behaviour was odd, to say the least.'

'How will we proceed?' asked Kate.

'You will be your charming self, and I'll be the inquisitive one.'

Before long we arrived at the Lone Dog Cellar Door Sales area. We walked in, bold as brass and took two tall stools near the bar. A staff member came to attend to us.

'Good morning,' she welcomed, 'Would you like to try white or red.'

I ran my eye down the wine list lying on the bar. 'The Angel's Breath Riesling sounds interesting. Could I try that? What about you, Kate?'

She was also looking down the wine list. 'I'd like to try the Mother's Milk Chardonnay,' she replied. She looked at the woman behind the bar. 'Is that a good choice?' she asked.

'You have chosen two of our very best whites. Just a moment.' She walked away, filled two tasting glasses with our choices and returned with a salesperson's smile on her face.

'We are running short of these two wines so I would advise you to order quickly.'

Nothing like the ticking clock approach to generate sales, I thought. *She has been well trained.* I suspected they still had plenty of these wines, but I admired her sales chatter.

We sniffed and sipped, looking for the special quality in these wines. I nodded my approval to the woman and looked at Kate. She also showed she liked the wine she had chosen.

'Before we buy, could we please try a red?'

'Certainly, Sir. Which one would you like to try?

'Which of these is your best Cabernet?'

'I would recommend the Lone Wolf Cabernet.'

'Is that your best Cabernet?' I asked.

'It is one of our very best reds, yes.'

'Good. I would like to try that one.'

'One for me too,' added Kate.

Our tasting glasses were soon in front of us. We sniffed, sipped, and rolled the wine around our mouths. It was a fine Cabernet.

'This is exceptionally good wine,' I commented to the salesperson. 'Do you ever have bad wine?'

She looked at me with surprise and shock. 'What kind of a question is that?'

'Your wines that we have tasted are very good, but it occurred to me that perhaps sometimes they don't turn out so well. My question really is, if a wine turns out badly, what would you do with it?'

'How should I know. Tip it down the sink, I suppose.'

'Not label it with someone else's label?'

'Take your foul mouth out of here now before I call the Manager,' she shouted. 'We don't have to be treated like this.'

'Call Nigel. I'd like to ask him the same question.'

'He's not here today. Please leave before I call the police.'

'Come on, Kate. We've outstayed our welcome.'

We walked out to the car.

'You were pretty rough on her. Why?'

'I want her to tell Nigel. I would like to see what his reaction will be. I'm sorry it upset you, but this is a dirty business, and we will only get results by stirring the pot and seeing what jumps out.'

'I guess you are right. I just don't like upsetting people who are only doing their job.'

'Would you rather not come with me. I don't want to upset you further.'

'I've come this far, and I will continue. I know you are just doing what you do best, solving crimes. Sean, I love you and I want to support you. I'll try not to be a wuss.'

'Would you like me to tell you when to block your ears?'

Kate laughed. 'That would be hilarious, but I think it might give the game away. No, just carry on as you know best.'

We decided to go to Top of the Hill winery and try to talk with Kurt. I couldn't see what he would gain from having Daybreak go down, but with crime you never know. We pulled the car up and walked into the Cellar Door Sales area. Steve was the only person there again.

'Hi, Steve,' I greeted.

'Hi, Sean and Kate. Lovely to see you both again. What can I get you?'

'Information, Steve. We'll leave the wine tasting for another time.'

'I'll help as much as I can,' he replied.

'Is Kurt here today?'

'No. He's gone to Sydney again. I think he is trying to get more wine sales.'

'You make some fine wine here, but do you ever have a batch that goes sour?

Steve looked at me. His sharp eyes bored into mine, attempting to read my mind. 'Of course we do. Everyone does from time to time. You can't always keep the bacteria from spoiling a batch. And in answer to your next question, we have never put Daybreak wine labels onto a bad wine.' He tightened his mouth, and I could see him tensing for a battle.

'Thank you, Steve. I expected that would be your answer, but I had to ask. We have a serious crime and a murder to solve and someone in the valley knows more about it than they are letting on.'

'Kurt has too many worries of his own to get mixed up in your problems,' said Steve.

'I understand and I'm sorry I had to ask, but we won't solve our problems by pussyfooting around. By the way, Alec is hoping desperately that you will leave Kurt and become his chief winemaker.'

Steve gasped. 'Is he serious?'

'As night follows day.'

'When does he want me to start?'

'Tomorrow would be good.'

'Wow! This is the break I've been waiting for. I can't do any more for Kurt. He is broken and this place is only days from closing down. I need to let Kurt know when he gets back tomorrow. Shall we say the day after tomorrow?'

'Done.' I held out my hand to shake his. 'Congratulations, Steve. You and Alec will work well together. He'll be over the moon when I tell him you are coming.'

We left Steve practically dancing around the room.

'You've made him very happy,' said Kate.

'He has the skills, the smarts, and the personality to become a great winemaker. He and Alec will be good for each other. Almost a marriage made in Heaven.' I grinned at my own joke. I knew it wasn't good for anyone to laugh at their own jokes, but sometimes I couldn't help myself.

Kate looked at me and laughed out loud. 'Sometimes I wonder about you.'

'Sometimes I wonder about myself,' I answered with a grin. 'But back to reality. We still need to visit Cynthia at Over the Edge winery.'

I turned the vehicle to head in her direction.

'I'll need all your antennae waving for this one. I'll be depending upon your woman's intuition.'

'I'm ready, but remember she is also a woman and will have her antennae waving as hard as mine.'

We pulled into Over the Edge winery, parked the car and headed towards the Cellar Door Sales area. I noticed a groundsman watching us.

'Hullo,' said Cynthia from behind the bar. 'Back again so soon. You must have liked my wine.'

'We did,' said Kate taking the lead. 'It was scrumptious.'

I smiled in agreement.

'How can I help you today?' she asked.

'We have a few questions for you today,' said Kate, continuing her lead.

'Fire away.'

'Do you ever have a batch of wine go off?' asked Kate.

'Being infected with bacteria do you mean?'

'I'm sorry. Did I use the wrong terminology?' she said with a slight fluster. 'Yes, I guess that is what I meant.'

I watched Cynthia's eyes closely as she replied to Kate. There was something in the high intensity of her vision that seemed to bore into Kate's head. For a moment, her eyes flicked to the doorway and gave a hardly perceptible nod. I swung around but nobody was there.

'Of course we do. Every winemaker has a bad batch sometimes.'

'What do you do with it?' I asked.

Her eyes swung to mine. Her intense gaze bored into my head. It seemed we were having a mental conversation quite distinct from the verbalised one. 'What every sensible winemaker does, put it in a still and condense it into pure alcohol. There's a good market for straight spirit.'

'Never put someone else's label on it?'

She took a deep breath and exhaled slowly. Her brow puckered in anger. 'NO!'

If she had a weapon, I knew I would be the target. I stepped back a pace to give me room to defend myself.

Her mood changed like magic. Suddenly she was the convivial host. 'Have a drink on the house,' she said. 'Red or white'.

'Thank you, but we have to go,' answered Kate. 'Come on, Sean. We'll be late for our next meeting.'

I nodded, knowing there was no next meeting, but turned and began walking to the door.

'Come back soon,' called Cynthia, cynicism rolling off her tongue like running honey.

I waved farewell as we escaped out the door.

'Guilty as charged,' I said as we entered the vehicle.

'I agree,' said Kate. 'We just need to prove it.'

I backed out of the car park and was surprised to find the brakes didn't hold as I began a turn to head for the gate. My awareness heightened. Why didn't the brakes grab when I pressed the foot pedal.

My thoughts returned to the groundsman and the slight nod from Cynthia. *Had we been got at? Were we meant to die on the way home?* Once we had left the property, I tried the brakes again. Nothing happened.

'Kate,' I said rapidly. 'The brakes are not working. I think the lines have been cut. We are meant to die on our way home. We will travel slowly and when we come to a downgrade, I will be using the gears to slow us down but keep your seat belt tight and hang on if I can't slow us enough to avoid a crash.'

'Is there anything I can do?' she asked through tightened lips.

'Pull the handbrake on hard if I can't slow us enough.'

'Won't that have been cut too?'

'Someone has probably cut through the brake fluid lines that operate the main brakes. The handbrake is a separate steel cable.'

She gritted her teeth. 'I'll do my best.'

'Good girl. Hang on. Here is our first downgrade.'

The car began to increase speed as we headed down the hill. I change back to third gear, second gear, first gear. The engine roared in protest, but our speed was reduced. I watched anxiously as I spotted the bend in the road at the bottom of the slope.

'Ready with the handbrake,' I yelled. I battled the steering wheel to convince it to turn the vehicle without hitting one of the gum trees on the road verge.

Kate hauled up the handbrake and it slowed us enough to stay on the road. Once around the corner, the road levelled out and we crawled along slowly in first gear.

'Call your dad,' I shouted to be heard above the engine noise. 'Get him to head this way as quickly as he can. We will also need a tow truck.'

Kate reached for her phone, called Alec, and asked him to come for us straight away and organise a tow truck.

We kept moving slowly until at last Alec's vehicle came into view. I chose a patch of soft groundcover and small trees and headed into it.

'Hold on tight and pull that handbrake,' I shouted.

The car headed into the bush and was slowly brought to a standstill.

We left the vehicle and hurried to Alec's car.

'Glad you got here so quickly,' I said as he jumped from the driver's seat.

'What happened?'

'Brakes were cut, I'm guessing. I want it checked by the police.'

'I've got a tow truck coming,' he said.

Almost as he spoke, a tow truck came over the nearest hill and slowed down. The driver immediately saw my car in the scrub. He turned his truck, backed into the scrub, and jumped out to attach chains. Within minutes the winch on the truck was hauling my vehicle onto the truck's tray. The driver secured the car with chains.

'Where to, mate?' he asked me.

'Daybreak Winery,' I answered. 'Follow us.'

We jumped into Alec's car, and he turned to head back. The truck followed us, keeping four vehicle lengths behind us all the way.

Once there, I jumped out to point to where he should leave my vehicle.

'Did you call Bob?' I asked Alec.

'Yes. He'll have forensic guys here within minutes. Come inside and have a coffee.'

We followed him in.

'We know which winery has been doing the dirty on us,' I said as the coffee machine heated. 'Cynthia is the guilty one. She practically admitted to the wine fraud, and I'm almost sure it was her groundsman who cut our brake lines. But I have no idea why she would be involved in fraud and murder. There must be a wealthy mover and shaker behind her.'

The police soon arrived and one of them clambered under my vehicle with a powerful torch and a camera. He soon climbed out and came over to me.

'Your brake lines have definitely been cut with something sharp, possibly garden secateurs. I've taken a few photos. We'll have to put the vehicle on a hoist to do an official inspection, but there is no doubt. You'll need Bob's clearance before doing any repairs.'

Chapter Twelve

'So, you think you've identified the winery that put Alec's labels on bad wine, Sean. But how is this winery linked to Mark's murder?' asked Bob when we met the next day. 'I can understand why they tried to murder you. You were pushing your nose too far into their business.'

'Sean tends to push his nose too far into lots of peoples' business,' remarked Ken, 'but the surprising thing is, he gets results and solves crimes.'

'Thanks, Ken, 'I said with a grin, 'but so far, I haven't pushed my nose in far enough to get the real villain. I have the feeling that someone with a lot of money is behind all this. I believe that someone else is pulling Cynthia's strings. I am sure she was the one who organised to put Alec's labels on shonky wine, but I can't see her organising a group of bikers to murder Mark. That is way out of her league in my opinion.'

'Let's get more evidence,' said Bob. 'We can't arrest her on just your say so. Until we get real evidence, we can't make a move. We'll bring the vehicle in and inspect the damage. When we have the results of a professional assessment, we'll conduct a full enquiry, starting at her winery. I suggest you don't make any more moves in her direction. We can't risk another murder attempt.'

'Okay, Bob,' I said. 'I don't want to be dead either. It would be so boring.'

'Can't have you pushing your nose into the business of the angels,' commented Ken.

I wrinkled my nose at Ken. He smiled.

* * *

'I'm taking more of our wine to the Gourmet Tasting Centre,' said Alec a few days later. 'It's the BIG tasting day and the wrap-up of the week. The speeches will be tonight, so this is our big moment.'

'Want some help?' I asked.

'Not now but I'll need your support tonight.'

I wandered into the kitchen where Angelo and his team were preparing their last meals for the week.

'Hi, Angelo. How has the week been for you?'

He smiled. 'It has been a heavy week but a good one. We've made some good contacts and many of the customers have raved about the food. Very satisfying.'

'You've done a great job. I'll mention that to your dad.'

'Just tell him I am worth twice the money he pays me,' he said with a grin.

'Are Maria and Alonzo free?' I asked.

'I can give them a few minutes off.'

Angelo stepped into the dining area and signalled to Maria and Alonzo. They hurried over to him and he whispered something. They came into the kitchen and walked over to me.'

'We have some information for you,' said Alonzo.

Maria took over. She spoke quietly and I listened intently. My face moved from surprise to amazement at the ability of this pair to find out detailed information from so far away. I shook their hands and complimented them for their detective work.

'How can I thank you?' I asked. 'You have done a great job of investigating this matter.'

'Uncle Marcello told us that you helped him when he needed it, and we are to help you as much as we can.'

'Thank you,' I said. 'A thousand thanks. I will tell him how helpful you have been.'

'We need to get back to work. There is lots to be done today.'

'Thank you again,' I said with a wide smile on my face as they turned and returned to their work.

I stood for some time digesting all the information. I took a notebook from my pocket and made notes so I wouldn't forget any of the story.

Back in the lounge, I found Ken sitting at a computer, checking his email from work. 'Boy, have I got a story for you? It's way more interesting than those dull emails.'

He looked up with a smile on his face. 'Anything could be more interesting than this dull office stuff. Fire away.'

I began telling him the story that Maria and Alonzo had unravelled. From time to time I checked my notes to make sure I got the whole story straight. His face moved from surprise to anger.

'So, tonight is the big reveal?' he asked.

I nodded.

'I'll ask Bob to have all his troops at the tasting centre,' said Alec. 'They should be able to make some arrests tonight and close down this terrible business.'

* * *

That evening we dressed up for the event. It would be the final occasion of the festival that so many people had worked hard for. It had been a huge success with so many visitors flooding the wineries and the public events. Tonight would be the wrap up speeches from the organisers.

The chairwoman of the organising committee stood on a stage at one end of the hall. She tapped on a microphone to gain attention. Conversations died and she began her list of thanks and compliments. She thanked the organisers and the wineries for their outstanding effort in making this event one of the best. Mention was made of some of the unusual but successful individual events. Her comments were met with ovation and cheering.

She then read a list of the awards won in each wine category, finishing by declaring that the judges had chosen Daybreak Cabernet Sauvignon as the wine of the week. 'The judges made special mention of the skill of the winemaker, Mark Brook,' she said, pausing.

This announcement was followed by loud cheering and clapping. I saw Alec's face change from surprise to excitement. We all joined in the celebration. We took it as a commemoration of Mark's winemaking skills and an appropriate epitaph.

She called for quiet again and said, 'Unfortunately there have been a couple of events that we regret. I would like to invite Alec Marchison, owner of Daybreak Winery to tell you about them.'

The crowd was surprised by this break from tradition.

Alec looked at us then moved to the microphone. 'I have two things to tell you. The first is that someone gained by deception a set of our Cabernet labels and attached them to poor quality wine. The intention was to distribute this shoddy wine to destroy our reputation. Luckily, we were able to find the wine, and the people responsible have been apprehended.'

Many of the audience had already heard the story. A number began to clap the successful outcome.

Alec continued, 'There was a much more serious event.' He began to choke up. 'Our winemaker, Mark Brook was... was... w...'

Kate poked me. 'Go and help him.'

She came with me as I moved forward and took the microphone from Alec. 'Alec's winemaker and close friend, Mark Brook, was callously murdered at the winery,' I said. 'The persons responsible for the murder are also locked up. The police did a fine job in identifying those responsible.'

I looked around the room seeing Cynthia and a well-dressed man beside her. My phone dinged as a text came in. I quickly checked it then handed the phone to Kate. I nodded at Ken, and she took the hint and moved down the hall to where Ken was standing.

She showed him the text. He moved to stand alongside Bob who was nearby and showed him the text.

Bob looked around with a worried expression on his face and waved over his senior officer. They had a whispered conversation then the senior moved to a group of policemen standing to one side. He gave whispered instructions, and they moved quietly through the crowd.

I continued, 'One of our local winery owners organised the gluing of Alec's wine labels onto bacteria infected wine.' I could see Cynthia tensing. 'She had been convinced by her brother to take part in this deception.'

All eyes turned to where Cynthia stood. She was the only female winery owner in the valley. The man standing next to her tensed and looked behind him to where his two minders stood. They flexed their arms, ready to intercede. The crowd began to shuffle backwards away from the woman, her brother and the two minders.

'But that is not all,' I continued. 'The brother organized some local thugs to carry out the wine hoax.

He organised for another group of thugs to murder Mark Brook.'

The brother swung around to his minders and shouted, 'Get him!'

The minders reached into their coat pockets, but before they could pull out revolvers, the police pounced on them, forced them to the floor and slapped handcuffs on them. Other police placed handcuffs on Cynthia and her brother.

'There is more,' I shouted into the microphone. 'He also found a way to bleed Kurt Weston at Top of the Hill winery dry through his son who has been attending a college in Sydney. This man got the son into heavy debt through gambling.'

The crowd was silent as I concluded. 'This man, a wealthy crook from Sydney, wanted his sister to win the major wine prizes at this event and the October wine show so he decided to wipe out the opposition.'

A slow handclap began as the police led the guilty people from the hall. I put my arm around Alec and led him from the microphone. Kate came and helped.

'Well done, Sean,' she whispered and sent me a silent air kiss.

Ken came across to us. 'Thanks for the tip about the bodyguards. Do you think I might be able to make use of your information sources? They are much better than mine.'

'Maybe next time,' I answered with a smile. I was sure there would be a next time.

Meet the Author

Ron Day holds many university degrees, including a PhD, and is a published author of a series of textbooks for use in primary, secondary, tertiary schools and colleges.

He has had more than 30 years' experience in teaching and writing.

He has recently turned his love of writing to include crime novellas. His first exciting crime novella, *Auditing Can Be Deadly* was released in 2021. This is the second book in his crime series.

Ron is available to do author talks, book signings or workshops on writing at schools, libraries or writing groups.

Contact info@morrispublishingaustralia.com for more information or to book.